THE ALMOND

THE ALMOND

Nedjma

Translated from the French
by

C. Jane Hunter

Grove Press
New York

This book was originally published in the French language under the title
L'amande by Plon, Paris.

Published simultaneously in Canada
Printed in the United States of America

FIRST EDITION

Library of Congress Cataloging-in-Publication Data

Nedjma.
    [Amande. English]
    The almond / Nedjma ; translated from the French by C. Jane Hunter.
      p. cm.
    ISBN 0-8021-1805-4
    I. Hunter, C. Jane. II. Title.

PQ2714.E45A7313 2005
843'.92—dc22

                              2004060867

Grove Press
an imprint of Grove/Atlantic, Inc.
841 Broadway
New York, NY 10003

05 06 07 08 09   10 9 8 7 6 5 4 3 2 1

THE ALMOND

Prologue

This narrative is first of all a story of soul and of flesh. Of a love that states its name, often crudely, and is not burdened by any moral standards other than those of the heart. Through these lines, in which sperm and prayer are joined, I have attempted to break down the walls that now separate the celestial from the terrestrial, body from soul, the mystical from the erotic.

Literature alone has the efficacy of a "lethal weapon." So I used it. Free, crude, and in exultation. My ambition is to give back to the women of my blood the power of speech confiscated by their fathers, brothers, and husbands. In tribute to the ancient Arab civilization in which desire came in many forms, even in architecture, where love was liberated from being sinful, in which both having and giving pleasure was one of the duties of the believer.

I raise these words as one raises a glass, to the health of Arab women, for whom recapturing the confiscated mention of the body is half the battle in the quest to healing their men.

Praise be to God who created the penis straight as a lance so it may wage war inside the vagina. . . . Praise be to Him who bestowed upon us the gift of nibbling and sucking lips, of placing thigh against thigh, and of laying our scrotum down at the threshold of the door of Compassion.

Cheikh O. M. Nefzaoui
The Perfumed Garden

By Way of a Response
to Cheikh Nefzaoui

I, Badra bent Salah ben Hassan el-Fergani, born in Imchouk under the sign of Scorpio, shoe size thirty-eight, and soon to reach my fiftieth year, make the following declaration: I don't give a damn that Black women have delectable cunts and offer total obedience; that Babylonian women are the most desirable and women from Damascus the most tender to men; that Arab and Persian women are the most fertile and faithful; that Nubian women have the roundest buttocks, the softest skin, and passion that burns like a tongue of fire; that Turkish women have the coldest wombs, the most cantankerous temperament, the most rancorous heart, and the most radiant acumen; and that Egyptian women are soft-spoken, offer kind-hearted friendship, and are fickle in their constancy.

I declare that I do not give a damn about sheep or fish, Arabs or Christians, the East or the West, Carthage or Rome, Henchir Tlemsani or the Gardens of Babylon, Galilee or Ibn Battouta, Naguib Mahfouz or Albert Camus, Jerusalem or Sodom, Cairo or Saint Petersburg, Saint John or Judas, foreskin or anus, virgins or whores, schizophrenics or paranoiacs, singers such as Ismahan or Abdelwahab, the Harrath Wadi or the Pacific Ocean, Apollinaire or Moutannabi, Nostradamus or Diop the Marabout.

For I, Badra, proclaim to be certain of one thing only: I am the one with the most beautiful cunt on earth, the best designed, the best developed, the deepest, warmest, wettest, noisiest, most fragrant and singing, the one most fond of cocks when they rise up like harpoons.

I can say it, now that Driss is dead and I have buried him beneath the wadi's laurels in heathen Imchouk.

I still long for a kiss sometimes, even today. Not one stolen between two doorways, hurried and clumsy, but slowly and peacefully given and received. A kiss on the mouth. A kiss on the hand. A bit of ankle, a detail of the temple, a perfume, an eyelid, a languid happiness, an eternity. From this time on, my fifty years are able to give birth. In spite of the menopausal hot flashes and pinnacles of rage. Smiling, I treat my ovaries as liars. Nobody knows I haven't made love in three years. Because I no longer have an appetite. I've left Tangiers to its own people. To German porno flicks picked up by satellite after midnight. To country bumpkins whose armpits smell and who puke up their beer in dark alleyways. To silly girls swishing their ass, who in chattering clusters get themselves picked up by a Mercedes stolen in Europe. To the imbeciles who wear the veil because they refuse to live in their time and are angling for paradise at half price.

I glance at young Safi from the corner of my eye. He is the day laborer who, perched on my very own tractor, is blatantly

coming on to me. He is just thirty years old and, illiterate that he is, must surely be thinking of the loot when he puts the make on me. Not mine, but that which Driss left me by legal bequest, dated August 1992. I've been wondering for two weeks now whether I shouldn't fire the boy, outraged as I am by his suspecting me of senile lustfulness and hoping to take advantage of that. But I change my mind as soon as I see his little girl, her braids full of ribbons, running toward him and kissing his unshaven cheek. I'll give him another week before I plug a volley of buckshot into his butt, just to put him in his place.

I know I'm unparalleled in bed, and that, were I to decide to take Safi on, I'd make him want to leave his wife and child. But that hick doesn't know what I know. That you fuck well only out of love, never for money, and that the rest is just performance. Love and experience it unswervingly. Love and lose; and wounded, accept that screwing serves as a stand-in when the heart falls from the highest peak and there is no net to protect it from its aerobatics. Crash and admit to living as an amputee. Since the head is intact.

Perhaps it is this fool of a Safi who pushed me into writing. To reason with my anger. To untangle the web. To relive my life and enjoy it a second time around instead of fantasizing about a new one. I started to scribble some things in a notebook. Street names, names of cities. Memories. Forgotten recipes.

One day I wrote, "The key to female pleasure is everywhere: nipples getting hard, frozen with desire, feverish and demanding. They need saliva and caresses. Biting and cajoling. Breasts awaken and ask only to let their milk spurt. They want to be suckled, touched, held, enclosed, and then set free. Their insolence knows no bounds. Nor does their magic spell. They melt in the mouth, they hide, harden, and focus on their pleasure. They want sex. As soon as they know the situation is right, they become openly lascivious. They envelop the cock and, reassured, grow bolder. Their nipples sometimes think they are a clitoris or even a penis. They come to lie in the folds of a discreet anus. Force the opening of a hole that, because it wants to inhale an object or a being, consumes everything that offers itself: a finger, a nipple, or a well-oiled dildo. The key lies wherever you must go, wherever you haven't thought of going: neck, earlobes, the fold of a hairy armpit, the part between the buttocks, toes that have to be tasted to know what loving means, the inside of thighs. Everything on the body is capable of frenzy. Of pleasure. Everything moans and flows for anyone who knows how to titillate. And drink. And eat. And give."

I blushed about what I had written, then found it to be very right. What is to stop me from continuing? The chickens are cackling in the courtyard, the cows are calving and giving lavish

milk, the rabbits fornicate and give birth every month. The world is turning. So am I. What should I be ashamed of?

"You, Arab woman," Driss used to say. The Arab woman is three quarters Berber and despises those who think she's good only for emptying chamber pots. I, too, watch television and could have been a Stephen Hawking if they had told me about quantum physics early on. Or given a concert in Cologne like Keith Jarrett, whom I just discovered. I might even have been a painter and exhibited at the Metropolitan Museum in New York. For I, too, am stardust.

"You, Arab woman." Of course, I am an Arab, Driss. Who better than an Arab woman would have known how to welcome you, any man, inside her womb? Who washed your feet, fed you, mended your burnooses, and gave you children? Who was on the lookout for you when you came home after midnight, brimful of wine and questionable jokes, then suffered your hasty assaults and your premature ejaculations? Who made sure your boys wouldn't screw around and your girls wouldn't get knocked up around the corner of a street or in an abandoned quarry? Who never said a word? Who reconciled wolf and sheep? Who steered the delicate course? Who went into mourning for you for twelve months straight? Who repudiated me? Who married and divorced me for the simple reason of safeguarding his ill-placed pride and his inherit-

ance interests? Who beat me up after every lost war? Who raped me? Who ripped me off? Who, besides me, the Arab woman, has had it up to here with an Islam you have distorted? Who, besides me, the Arab woman, knows you are deep in the shit and it serves you right, you and that mealy-mouthed mug of yours? So why shouldn't I speak of love, of soul and ass, if only to match your unjustly forgotten ancestors in the argument?

In the guiblia *room, Driss had piled up his boxes of books, his illuminated manuscripts, his masterpiece paintings, and his stuffed wolves with their empty gaze. Since his death, only young Sallouha is authorized to go in there once a week to dust the office and fill a small Chinese porcelain pot with fresh ink. I hardly ever entered there, as Driss's things were familiar but totally unnecessary to me.*

When I decided to write my life story, I opened the boxes with books in search of the thick and very old Arabic volumes from which Driss used to fish up his clever sayings and his few bits of wisdom. I knew that I would come across crazier, braver, and more intelligent folks than I am.

I read. And reread. As soon as I felt I was out of my depth, I would go to the fields. I'm a woman of the land. Only the breath of the wheat and the smell of seed could straighten out my entangled threads.

Then I came back to the ancient writers, amazed at their daring that has no equal among their twentieth-century descendants, who, for the most part, are devoid of honor and humor. Mercenary and spineless, besides. I would pause each time an idea struck me by its accuracy or a phrase choked me with its quiet vigor. I have to admit that sometimes I laughed out loud, just as I was startled by my sense of modesty at other times. But I decided to write in a similar vein: freely, informally, with a clear head and a quivering sex.

After eight hours of travel, which came of no sudden impulse, I got off in Tangiers. Like a drunken hearse, my life was heading straight for disaster, and to save it I had had no choice but to jump on the train that leaves the Imchouk station every morning at four o'clock sharp. For five years I had been hearing it arrive, blow its whistle, and leave without having the courage to cross the street and step over the station's low railing to put an end to contempt and corruption once and for all.

Feverish and my heart on tenterhooks, I didn't sleep a wink all night. Noises dotted the passing of the hours, sounding the same: Hmed's coughing and spitting, the barking of the two dogs—both mutts—that stand watch in the courtyard, and the hoarse song of some absent-minded rooster. Before the call to the early Morning Prayer, I was up, wrapped in a cotton *haïk* that I had ironed two days earlier at the home of Arem, my neighbor and dressmaker, the only woman in a radius of thirty kilometers who owns a charcoal iron. I grabbed my bag, which I had stuffed inside a couscous jar, patted the

snouts of the dogs, who came to sniff at me, crossed the street and the embankment in two great strides, and jumped into the last car, pretty much plunged in darkness.

My brother-in-law had taken it upon himself to buy my ticket, and Naïma, my sister, had managed to get it to me by hiding it in a stack of cookies. The conductor, who came to check the compartment, punched it with lowered eyes, not daring to stop and stare at me. He must have confused me with Uncle Slimane's new wife, who wears veils and prides herself on copying city women. Had he recognized me, he would have forced me to get off and called the family-in-law, who would have drowned me in a well. In the evening, he will tell the news to his friend Issa, the teacher, while chasing away the flies that flit about his glass of cold and bitter tea.

The compartment remained just about empty until we reached Zama, where the train stopped for a good fifteen minutes. A fat gentleman came in, a *bendir* by his side, with two women in blue and red *melias* covered in tattoos and jewelry. Their mouths hidden behind their *ajars,* they began whispering to each other, bursting out in soft laughter, then raised their voices, emboldened by the absence of any unknown men. Before long, the musician took a flask from the pocket of his djellaba, had three swigs without taking a breath, and stroked his bendir at length before playing a jaunty and slightly impudent little melody that I had often heard the nomads sing while harvesting.

The women began to dance, winking at me vulgarly as they skimmed the musician's torso with the fringes of their rainbow-colored belts every time they moved their hips. My sullen look must have annoyed them, because they ignored me for the rest of the trip.

I was entertained every second of the way up to Medjela, where, rowdy and dead drunk, the trio got off, probably to celebrate a wedding of some rich kinsman.

I had to travel two more hours by bus to reach Tangiers. The city could be recognized by its cliffs, its white facades, and the masts of its docked ships. I wasn't hungry or thirsty. I was just scared. Of myself, to be precise.

It was a bleak Tuesday with nothing but *ajajs,* sandstorms that brings migraine and jaundice as only the month of September can. I had what seemed like a fortune on me, thirty dirhams, and could easily have hailed one of the green and black taxis that crisscross the smart streets of Tangiers, a city that appears cold, no matter what my older brother used to say when he returned to the village, laden with fabrics for my father. I always suspected Habib of lying in order to embellish things and act like everyone else from Imchouk, given to fantasizing, lots of wine and whores. In the Judgment Book that the Eternal One keeps, men are surely listed in the chapter on blowhards.

I did not take a taxi. I had Aunt Selma's address clumsily scribbled on a bit of graph paper, ripped from the notebook of Abdelhakim, my nephew, who before my wedding night

THE ALMOND

had rolled onto the conjugal bed to ward off fate and induce me to give an heir to my skunk of a husband.

As I stepped out of the bus, I staggered a little, blinded by the sun and the clouds of dust. A porter, sitting cross-legged under a poplar tree, watched me with a stupid look, his fez filthy and his muffler stained with the juice of chewing tobacco. I asked him the way, sure that a poor man couldn't harm a veiled woman or allow himself to bother her.

"The rue de la Vérité, you say? Well, I don't really know, cousin!"

"I was told it was very close to Mouley Abdeslam."

"That isn't far from here. Go up the boulevard, and you'll pass the Grand Socco and enter the Medina. Surely someone there will be able to help you find the right street."

He was from the country, a blood brother, and his rural accent warmed my heart. In Tangiers, too, they spoke the patois of the isolated villages. I moved away hesitantly and took a few steps roughly in the direction the porter had indicated, when a young man dressed in blue overalls and matching fez blocked my way, looking very pleased with himself.

"Don't be afraid. I overheard you asking the porter for directions to Hasouna. I live in that area and could take you to the address you're looking for. Tangiers is a dangerous city, you know, and women as beautiful as you should never walk alone."

Caught by surprise and completely thrown by his audacity, I didn't know what to say. With two-thirds of my face

14

concealed by my veil, I glared at him, feeling offended. He burst out laughing.

"Don't look at me that way, or I'll drop dead on the spot. You've just come from the country. Anyone can tell that from a hundred miles away. I'm only going to accompany you. I can't let an *ouliyya* wander around Tangiers without any protection. You don't need to answer, just follow me and *alik aman Allah,* God will protect you."

Not having any choice, I followed him, telling myself that I could always scream if he made a move, rouse all the passersby, or call to one of the traffic cops all dressed in their tightly fitted uniforms with shiny leather stripes. Actually, I wasn't all that scared. Having the guts to take the train to get away from my husband reduced every other act of brazenness to child's play.

I glanced furtively at the man preceding me and found him to cut a fine figure. About my age and with the gait of a strutting rooster. He never once turned around, but I could sense that he was aware of my contented gazing at his broad shoulders, fascinated as I was with his virility. A strange feeling coursed through my veins: the pleasure of braving the forbidden in a city where I knew no one and no one knew me. I even told myself that freedom was more intoxicating than springtime.

I had a hard time keeping my eyes on my guide, for the streets seemed so wide to me and their plane trees so imposing. Cafés everywhere had men in djellabas or western clothes sitting on the terraces. More than once I felt my legs tremble under the insistent looks that lifted my veil, which was the color of fresh

butter and worn the urban way. Tangiers may have impressed me with its buildings, but its men seemed in every respect to be exactly the same as those I'd left behind in Imchouk to get bogged down in dung, quibbling over everything.

After walking for twenty minutes, the man turned left, then ducked into an alley. It was a narrow passageway that kept going up and winding around. Suddenly, I was thirsty in that dark back street following a guide whose name I didn't even know.

Having reached the entrance to the Medina, he stopped. It was light again, and, other than the distant echo of Koranic verses being intoned by a chorus of children, the silence was complete. Without turning around, my guide said:

"Here we are. What house is it you're looking for?"

I handed him the crumpled piece of paper I held clutched in my hand. He looked at it for a long time and then exclaimed:

"Well, now, here it is, here on your right!"

Had I really arrived at my destination? I was suddenly filled with doubt. The door my guide was pointing out might hide an ambush, a lair in which thugs would drug me, abuse me, decapitate me, and then throw me into the "grottos hewn in the cliffs" or the creeks that "stink worse than any of the polecats at home could ever do," as my brother Habib would assert.

The man surmised my discomfort.

"Do you have a name or only an address? Someone we could call?"

Hopefully, I whispered:

"Aunt Selma."

He pushed open the heavy studded front door and disappeared into a dark entryway. I heard him yell at the top of his lungs, "*Ya oumalli ed-dar,* hello! Anyone at home here?"

The shutters of a window snapped open above my head, a door creaked, and unfamiliar, slightly smothered voices could be heard.

"Is there an Aunt Selma here?"

A murmur, hasty footsteps, and, worried, my aunt appeared in her fine pink mules, chiseled like a piece of jewelry. She slapped herself hard on the chest:

"Oh! And what are *you* doing here?"

At least she was really here, and that was all that mattered to me. My guide emerged from behind her back, happy and quite proud that he had tracked her down. I felt like laughing.

"What's happened to you? Did someone die, down there in the village?"

Without thinking and very candidly, I answered:

"I did."

She quickly recovered and, intrigued, looked at my guide, then thanked him for his kindness. It seemed to me as if my answer had amused the young man, who adjusted his cap, crossed his arms, and said to my hostess, "Mission accomplished, Lalla. Just a word of advice: With eyes like hers, don't ever let this gazelle out of your sight." He smiled. He left. He had already taken possession of my head.

Aunt Selma was in the middle of a gathering of women when I disturbed her. Later on, I learned that in Tangiers the afternoon was the time for women to congregate. All dressed up, fashionable and lighthearted, they'd meet around platters filled with pastries to sip their coffee or tea, try a Spanish or an American cigarette, exchanging their off-color jokes, gossip, and only half-sincere confidences. These *ichouiyyates* were a most serious social ritual, almost as important as the *frouates*—the stiff and formal evenings when weddings, circumcisions, and engagements were celebrated, where one had to display one's most beautiful finery and never appear to be either poor or cast aside by one's husband.

She got me settled in a clean bedroom, lit an oil lamp, and apologized for having to leave me by myself.

"You understand, don't you, that I have people waiting for me upstairs next door?"

She put a pitcher of water and a glass on the table and told me that she wouldn't be long. I drank the water in large gulps straight from the pitcher and, exhausted as I was, fell asleep

right away. It was the vision of the man in blue overalls that rocked me before I fell into a deep dream-filled sleep, striped in gray and yellow like an autumnal storm.

I awoke starving in the middle of the night, my head propped on a bolster and a woolen blanket thrown over my legs. The couch was narrow and hard, and the sounds in the house were unfamiliar. The bundle I had packed with fresh bread and two hard-boiled eggs was lying by my feet. Hunger is stronger than fear. With my eyes closed, I devoured my bit of food in the oval-shaped room with the huge, hostile shadow of the furniture projected on its walls and its ceiling much higher than those in Imchouk.

Keeping myself from having any thoughts, I fell back asleep. I was in Tangiers. Having left me with nothing to hold on to, the twenty years behind me mattered little. My past was the past. It was moving away as the hail-encumbered clouds move away, hurriedly and guilt ridden. But Imchouk was present, radiating its full light. In my dreams, I am always running in bare feet and cutting across the barley and alfalfa fields to get away from my playmates, hair dotted with poppies and laughing brightly.

Imchouk is both stupid and strange at the same time. As plain as platitude itself and more askew than the caves of Djebel Chafour that on its western side leave it open to the winds and the black and cracked gravel stone of the desert. Only two steps away from hell, the waxy and pagan greenery that blazes there seems to scoff at the threatening sand

laying siege to its orchards. The houses there are low and white, their narrow windows painted ochre. A minaret rises in the center, not far from the Bar of the Misunderstood, the only place where the men can curse and vomit in public.

The Harrath Wadi has traced a slit through Imchouk that divides the town into two facing quarter moons. When I was little, I would often sit among the luscious laurel trees, that billow bitter and deceitful on its banks so I could watch the mocking and misleading waters flow. Like the men of Imchouk, the Harrath Wadi likes to strut around, compulsively trampling everything in its path. Its shimmering water, made muddy and foaming by the autumn floods, coils through the village before it gets lost in the valley far away.

"That wadi is indecent," Uncle Slimane's other wife, Taos, would roar. At the time I had no idea what decency was, since all I saw around me were roosters jumping their chickens and stallions penetrating their fillies. Later on, I understood that this affliction of decency was imposed on women only to make them into painted mummies with empty eyes. Calling the wadi indecent resonated a rage that wordlessly criticized Imchouk for its fertile womanly lustfulness. Imchouk drives the shepherds crazy and makes them mount the first thing that reminds them of a female rump, including a donkey's vagina and a nanny goat's hole.

I have always loved the Harrath Wadi. Perhaps because I was born in the year of its most horrendous flood. It had overflowed its bed, inundated the houses and shops, stuck its

tongue right down into the interior courtyards and the wheat reserves. Fifteen years later, as we sat in the courtyard of her vine-covered house that Uncle Slimane had paved with marble to let his wife know how much he loved her, Aunt Selma told me about the episode. Her delightful cleavage pleased the girl that I still was, whose breasts were just beginning to show beneath her weightless dresses. Aunt Selma would talk and, between two moments of laughter, crack the green, harsh almonds with a quick blow of a yellow copper mortar. She loved the summer for the abundance of its fruit that would be piled up in the entryway in large wicker baskets the farmers had brought directly from the orchards.

"That year, we were cut off from the rest of the world for twenty-one days," she remembered. "And the world couldn't have cared less for this grimy armpit of the earth! What a honeymoon! I would've been better off waiting, nice and dry, at my mother's house until the November storms were over!" she added as she burst out laughing. "But I was a dummy and your uncle was impatient. Can you imagine my face when I turned up in this dump in a silk caftan and spike heels? Did you know that the farmers' wives used to walk for miles to come and gape at me as if I were some sort of exotic animal? They'd pull at my hair to be sure I wasn't a doll. I tell you, this really is the sticks here!"

She handed me a fistful of white almonds, then rekindled the fire in the brazier with her fan. The tea was humming, spreading its heavy, sweet scent.

"The flood gave those sanctimonious cousins of yours a fever and hallucinations," Aunt Selma began again. "Tidjani, the myopic one, and Ammar, the legless cripple, decided that so much water could only be a good sign: It stirs up the soil and, in passing, cleanses our sinful hearts. Sin! That's the only word they know! As if we weren't Muslims, spending our days crapping in the wheat! Those cretins think they are the Mufti of Mecca because they recite three Koranic verses over the corpses before they, too, will be put in a hole. May their faces be covered with smallpox! As for the rest of these jerks, they all went off to tell the world the flood had come to announce the end of time. Bullshit! As long as Gog and Magog keep their noses clean, as long as that shady character of an Antichrist still hasn't turned up in Jerusalem, and Jesus, Mary's son, has not come back to put some order into this cosmic mess, we can sleep peacefully! We can be sure that God has had it with our cruelty, but He has yet to decide to chase us out of His lovely Eden with some good kicks in the butt! Because you can rest assured that Eden is down here, and we'll never have another one this beautiful, not even in the highest heavens! May God forgive us for our nastiness and our stupidities!"

I almost peed in my pants with laughter at Lalla Selma's talent for sarcastic remarks and blasphemous images. She had managed, I don't know how, to inherit the knowledge of an illustrious uncle who was a theologian, and she had no equal in sticking everyone with a nickname and thereby making that

person the laughingstock of the town. Just as she was the only one who could yell at God without ever losing respect for Him.

Frowning and with a thoughtful look, she added:

"You know what? I don't believe in sin. And, on Judgment Day, those who revel in that word will have nothing to show to the holy gaze of the Master of the world but their scabby dicks as their one and only hideous sin. They think that the vile acts they committed with that bit of flesh are going to impress Him! Well, I'm telling you that all those bastards will rot in hell for not having committed any fine and noble sins, worthy of the infinite grandeur of the Almighty God!"

When lashing out at the people of Imchouk, Aunt Selma always said "they" meaning the men; she never used "they" as the plural for *she*. As if the escapades of women were just inconsequential things meant to make the constellations laugh.

Confused, I took it upon myself to ask her what a fine and noble sin would be. She gave her dazzling lioness laugh, taking the bottle away from the brown puppy she had been feeding and that wouldn't stop licking her feet. Suddenly solemn and dreamy, she murmured:

"Loving, my girl. Just loving. But it is a sin that deserves Paradise as a reward."

Aunt Selma was born in Tangiers. Arriving in Imchouk on the arm of Uncle Slimane one fine day, she saw a flooding wadi for the first time in her life. Fair and buxom, she picked up the basket that was my cradle and without further ado kissed the magnificent baby that I was, under the nervous look of my father who was not used to that kind of effusion.

Now she and I had settled down beneath the canopy on the patio with its chipped green tiles, and it was as if we were all alone in the world, beyond time, beyond Tangiers. She smiled again at the memory of her arrival in Imchouk, naive and completely out of place, and the welcome my visibly annoyed father had held in store for her.

"Because of the wadi?" I asked.

"No, of course not! Because of you! Another mouth to feed just as times were getting harder and your mother, after a five-year pause, seemed to be starting to give birth again like a rabbit ."

I told her that my father had never made me feel I was a burden.

"With good reason! You were his favorite. Your father was a softy but had to hide his sensitive nature under a big pile of surly silences. It's not always fun being a man, you know! You're not supposed to cry. Even when you're burying your father, your mother, or your child. You're not supposed to say I love you, or that you're afraid or you've caught the clap. No wonder with all of that that our men become monsters."

I do believe that was the only time I ever saw Aunt Selma show any compassion for men.

As I was playing with the crumbs of sesame cake she had put next to my cup, I never stopped looking at her face, surreptitiously, dreading there might be some sign of reluctance or irritation. No, it seemed Aunt Selma didn't hold it against me that I had landed in her house without alerting her first. She had let me come out of my sleep gently, content to just smoke and sip her glasses of tea, evoking her memories of Imchouk only to help me open my heart to her, which she inferred was chained down with hatred and anger. Once she gave up on hearing me broach the subject head-on, she plopped her arms firmly on her belly, twiddled her thumbs, and went on the attack:

"Fine, and now tell me what you're doing here. I hope you didn't set the house on fire or poison your mother-in-law. I'd better admit it right away: That marriage never did seem right to me at all. I know one should settle down but not at that price!"

I lowered my head. If I wanted to be honest with her, I owed it to myself to tell her everything in detail. But I was in pain over so many things that I simply wanted to erase them from my memory forever.

Badra's Marriage

Hmed was forty. I had just turned seventeen. But he was a notary, and the title, which made them exist on the registers of the state, gave him inordinate power in the eyes of the villagers. He had already been married twice and repudiated his wives for reasons of sterility. He had the reputation of being gloomy and irascible; he lived on a lovely family property situated at the edge of the village not far from the railroad station. Everyone knew that he provided his future wives with an exorbitant dowry and arranged a lavish wedding for them. He was one of the best catches in Imchouk and coveted by the good virgins and their grasping mothers.

One day, Hmed's mother opened the door of our house, and I knew immediately that it was my turn to put my head on the block. I had overheard one farmer's wife whispering to my mother and giving her the advice of a feigned ally:

"Just accept! Your daughter is already a woman. You can't continue to let her go to the city and pursue those damned

studies, which won't do her any good, anyway. If you keep being so hardheaded, she'll get so itchy that she'll leave and start chasing after men."

True, *studying didn't mean much to me, but being locked up back home wasn't a cheerful prospect, either. The first and only middle school for girls in Zrida was my safe conduct pass to get outside our walls, and boarding school, in particular, gave me the chance to get away from my brother Ali's supervision. My youngest brother was a real cockerel who put his honor in the pants of the tribe's females and who had been officially appointed as my guardian after my father's recent death. Ordering women around allows boys to assert themselves as masculine and virile. Without a sister close by to beat to a pulp, their authority dwindles and atrophies like a pecker in need of arousal.*

My future mother-in-law didn't wait for my mother's definitive agreement to begin judging me and sizing up my abilities as a prospective wife worthy of her clan and her son. One day, she appeared with her oldest daughter at the hammam when I was there. They examined me from top to bottom, feeling my breasts, my behind, my knees, and finally the curve of my calf. I felt like a sheep for the religious holiday of Eid. All that was missing were the feast's ribbons. But, knowing the rules and customs, I let them handle me without bleating. Why interfere with the well-oiled codes that change the hammam

into a souk where human flesh is sold at a third of the price of regular meat?

Then came the grandmother's turn to come through the door of our family home. She was a hundred years old, with tattoos from forehead to toes. She sat down in the courtyard and watched me attend to the household chores as she spat the juice of her chewing tobacco into a large blue and gray checked handkerchief. My mother didn't stop watching me, urging me to do my very best, knowing the old shrew would report to her family in full on my talents as a housewife. As for me, I knew the goods weren't what they were supposed to be.

Hmed had known me since I was a tiny girl and had been watching me with smoldering eyes for the past two years every time I left for or came home from school. He saw me walking, my eyes down and moving along fast, in a hurry to flee voyeuristic looks and spiteful tongues. He decided I was a pretty hole to dive into and that it was a good deal to make. He wanted children. Only boys. To penetrate me, to make me pregnant, and then parade around at the parties of Imchouk, his chest thrown out and his head high, proud to have ensured himself of male progeny, would please him.

In the winter of 1962, I was no longer at my school desk but bent over tablecloths to be embroidered, cushions to be stuffed, woolen blankets whose pattern I was to choose so they

could be added to my trousseau. I had finer dreams than some-one like Hmed as a prince charming and certainly younger than he. I was ashamed I had let them break my will with such ease. Just to say no to negate the horrible masquerade, I began to wear shapeless qamis *and put my hair up under the first rag I found on the laundry line. I disgusted myself.*

The middle school was far away, and the memory of my schoolmates, among them the beautiful Hazima, was begin-ning to fade. The outside world came to me in a mutter through the news on the radio. Neighboring Algeria was independent, the FLN victorious. It made the little simpleton Bornia dance in the streets like a female satyr. Her big feet in their heavy clogs kept the beat of her triumph on the chalky ground of the marketplace.

I didn't leave the house except to go to Arem, the seamstress. On my way there, I would carefully skirt the house of the hajjalat. *Passing alongside the walls of the Farhat girls could be a risky thing for women and might cost them dearly. But I had already dared take a look at more private things than their house, and the raw memory I had of it sniggered slyly at the nose of Imchouk the strict.*

My imminent marriage secured me some privileges. A young peasant girl replaced me in the household, for there was no ques-tion anymore of me spoiling my hands by washing the tile floor,

spinning wool, or kneading bread. I was living like a female sheik—no chores to do, no orders to follow. I could eat the most sumptuous meals, and the best piece of meat was mine by right. I was to attain a respectable plumpness before I could enter the marital bed. They filled me with creamy sauces, with couscous sprinkled with sman, *and with* baghrir *smothered in honey. Not to mention the pastries stuffed with dates or almonds or, a great luxury, the* tagines *with pine nuts, a rare commodity. I gained a pound of fat a day, and my mother was delighted with my rosy and chubby cheeks.*

Then they cloistered me in a dark room. Since no sun was to touch me, my skin grew pale and white under the approving glances of the women of my clan. A light skin is a privilege of the rich, as being blond is of the Europeans and the Central Asian Turks, descendants of the deys, the beys, and especially the janissaries, those mercenaries Driss later told me about with consummate disdain.

Then they forbade me any visits, for fear of the evil eye. I was queen and slave at the same time. The object of every attention and the last to feel concerned about what was happening around me. The females of the clan were preparing me for immolation while they murmured quietly to me that it is up to women to seduce the hearts of men. "And their bodies, too!" whispered Neggafa, Imchouk's official hair remover. My sister

replied maliciously: "And a man who doesn't succeed in seducing his wife? What, when all is said and done, is he worth?"

Finally, the wedding day arrived. Neggafa came to our house early in the morning. She asked my mother whether she wanted to check the "thing" with her.

"No, go ahead, do it by yourself. I trust you," my mother answered.

I think that my mother was looking to spare herself the embarrassment that such a "check" never fails to arouse, even among the most hardened madams. I knew to what examination I had to submit and was getting ready for it, my heart flooded and my teeth clenched with rage.

Neggafa asked me to lie down and take my panties off. Then she spread my legs and bent down over my genitals. I suddenly felt her hand move the two lips apart and a finger go in. I did not cry out. The examination was short and painful, and its burning stayed with me like a bullet received right in the face. I only wondered whether, before raping me in all impunity, she had washed her hands.

"Congratulations!" Neggafa called out to my mother, who had come to get the news. "Your daughter is intact. No man has touched her."

I thoroughly detested both my mother and Neggafa, accomplices and assassins.

"Ah, yes!" Aunt Selma sighed. "To think that we're still moldering in caves while the Russians are firing rockets off into space and the Americans are claiming they're going to the moon! But consider yourself lucky. In the Egyptian countryside, the *dayas,* with a handkerchief twisted around their finger, deflower the virgins for their husbands. It seems that over there they even cut everything away from the women. What they walk around with between their legs is a true catastrophe. For hygienic reasons, so those pagans claim. Since when does dirt bother vultures? Pfff!"

Beside herself, Aunt Selma exploded. As for me, I was trying to imagine what a woman's sex would look like when its contours had been butchered. A shiver of horror ran down my back, from my neck to my buttocks.

"I'll tell you something," my aunt continued. "They should bump them off, those brothers of ours who are like that, exactly as the Tunisians did. Look at their Bourguiba! He didn't beat about the bush. Hop! Out of the house with women, let them emancipate themselves! Swear you'll go out in the open

air. You'll go to school, by twos, by fours, by the hundreds! Now there's a man. A real man. And besides, he has blue eyes, and I love the sea."

Then, catching herself:

"And so? Hurry up and tell me the rest because I need to start cooking. Or else you'll faint with hunger before it is noon."

No, I didn't love Hmed, but I did think he'd be of use to me, at least—he'd make a woman of me. Free me and cover me with gold and kisses. All he managed to do was deprive me of my laughter.

He would come home stiffly every evening at six o'clock with his civil registers under his arm. He would kiss his mother's hand, barely say hello to his sisters, wave to me warily, and settle down in the courtyard to have his dinner.

I would serve him, then clear the table. Join him in the conjugal bedroom. Open my legs. Not budge. Not sigh. Not vomit. Feel nothing. Die. Stare at the Kilim carpet nailed to the wall. Smile at Saïed Ali decapitating the ogre with his forked sword. Wipe myself between the legs. Sleep. Hate men. Their thing. Their nasty-smelling sperm.

My sister Naïma was the first one to be suspicious: It wasn't going well between Hmed and me. Blushing, she tried to show me how to glean a few crumbs from the table of male

37

pleasure. I rebuffed her, unsatisfied woman that I was and incapable of saying so. And every evening, except when I had my period, I continued to spread my legs for a forty-year-old billygoat who wanted children and couldn't have any. I was not allowed to wash myself after our sinister frolics—the day after the wedding, my mother-in-law had ordered me to keep the "precious seed" inside me so I would get pregnant.

As precious as it may have been, Hmed's seed bore no fruit whatsoever. I was his third wife, and, like the first two, my belly continued to be barren, worse than a fallow field. I would dream of brambles growing in my vagina so that Hmed would scrape his thing on them and give up on coming back.

Aunt Selma was listening with a worried frown. My words were explicit and were growing bolder as I told her about the wretched life I'd led, made even more unbearable by the mask of secrecy I was forced to wear. I would never have imagined that I'd be conversing with her openly about my body and its frustrations. For the first time in my life, I was speaking to her as an equal, a woman now, after having been her very young niece for such a long time. She knew it, remarked on her age and mine, and accepted the sting of time, second to that of the inconstant and careless male. Feeling tender and close to her, I admired the still firm breasts of the more than forty-year-old woman she was, her satin skin, and I thought of the women of Imchouk who used to come and admire her from afar. How could Uncle Slimane have trampled on such opulence, and, above all, how could he have kissed all of this good-bye?

For three years, my belly was the main topic of every conversation and every quarrel. They checked my appearance, my food, my gait, and my breasts. I even caught my mother-in-law examining my sheets. It certainly wasn't my fluid that ran the risk of staining them, since my sources had dried up before they could even flow.

A child! A boy! The words alone made me want to commit infanticide. After three months of marriage, they forced me to drink brews of bitter herbs and sips of urine, to straddle the tombs of saints, to wear amulets that had been scribbled on by fqihs *with trachoma-burned eyes, to smear nauseating concoctions on my belly that made me puke under the fig tree in the garden. I hated my body, stopped washing, shaving, and perfuming it. As an adolescent, I could never get enough of your crystal perfume bottles, Aunt Selma, promising myself that I would sprinkle rose water and musk all over myself, from my head to my private parts, once I was as tall as a poplar tree.*

And then working hard. From sunup to sundown. And cooking. Until I hated the smell and taste of food. And then languish and rot, exhausted, while young brides would go from party to party, go off to welcome springtime in the fields as far as the first sand dunes and on their way back play in the luminous joyful orchards.

My mother, whom I went to see from time to time, was wrong about the nature of my distress. She thought I was desperate because I hadn't become pregnant and was lamenting "the laziness of my belly." Naïma just hugged me in silence, very tightly. She smelled of happiness, insolent and juicy.

One day my sister lost her temper and, furious, her eyes like lightning, cried out:

"It's his fault. You're not his first wife, and you won't be the last. He could deflower a hundred virgins and still wouldn't sire as much as a green onion for a son. So stop eating your heart out and tormenting yourself about your belly."

I blew up.

"I don't want any children, and I refuse to be pregnant!"

"Are you doing this on purpose then?"

"No! I let things happen, that's all."

"You know, you're hiding something. Is your husband . . . normal?"

"What's that supposed to mean, normal? He gets it up. It spews. It goes slack. Of course he's normal!"

Finally, Naïma understood and stammered pathetically:

"Well, then, make some effort to have your share. Pleasure, too, can be learned."

The word having been uttered, there was an embarrassed silence for a few moments. For the first time, Naïma was speaking straightforwardly of things sexual. But she seemed to have forgotten what my wedding night had been like, the horrors of the first time.

I never had my share of pleasure. Hmed, desperate about not seeing my belly grow round, at last no longer touched me. His sisters quickly guessed at the rift and pursued me with their sarcastic and hurtful remarks.

"So, how's the sterile one? Hmed doesn't want to hump you anymore?"

"Your vagina must be like a sieve. It can't hold on to any semen!"

Or else, "If your ass is as sullen as your face, it's no wonder your man runs away from you."

I sought refuge in my mother's house more than once, but after a week she would firmly show me the door.

"Your place is not with me anymore. You have a house and a husband. Accept your fate like the rest of us."

What did "like the rest of us" mean? That she had been raped by my father and taken against her liking and her will as well? I don't want to belong to a tribe that ends up in the sewer, with a mutilated heart and mutilated genitals like the Egyptian women, Aunt Selma! I said so to Naïma, and she did not protest. She even helped me to escape.

Aunt Selma lit a Kool, her fifth cigarette that morning, and looked at me with half-closed eyes, her index finger authoritatively.

"Fine, so now you've gotten rid of that old jerk who farts in bed instead of satisfying you. May God forgive those who were so blind as to put you in the hands of someone so inept. Oh, there's much more to be said about what you've told me. But there's no rush. We'll talk about it more later on. Now you're going to get some rest. Get your strength back. Forget all this."

Right thereafter she began again.

"Tell me, though, that young rascal who brought you here yesterday, where do you know him from?"

I related the facts to her, which she undoubtedly interpreted as my first "adventure" in Tangiers. She crushed out her cigarette on one of the brazier's legs.

"I bet you he'll come back to hang around the house as early as this afternoon! The eye of the cat won't let a juicy bit escape!"

I felt like washing up and told her so. She put a large pot on the kerosene stove that sputtered and spat before its long, foul-smelling yellow flame turned blue, then changed to an incandescent red. She set down a large basin in the kitchen.

"Today, you'll wash yourself here, but soon I'll take you to the hammam. You'll see how different it is from the Turkish baths down there."

In this "down there," vexation resounded that all the intervening years gone by had not managed to overshadow. After Uncle Slimane, Aunt Selma must have lived with a deeply scarred heart.

She then showed me the toilet in the corner.

"You'll be constipated for a day or two. Changing location always does that, but at least you'll know where to go. And don't pay any attention to that big trap in the corner. The rats are driving me crazy. They come from the sewers at night, but, may God catch them by the tail, they go wild over cheese! That lets me punish them right where they're misbehaving!"

Under the hot water, I felt lighthearted and luxuriant for the first time in ages. With eyes closed, my hands ventured to gently touch my shoulders and my hips. Joyous, the water trickled down to my pubis, and my nipples grew tense beneath the slight bite of the air.

Aunt Selma was right about my guide. He came back not just once but about fifty times, pacing up and down the alley, perky at first, then more and more contrite. He was insistent until, beside herself, my aunt allowed him in the door, whereupon he stood, awkwardly and with his cap askew, in the middle of the marble patio, whose blue veins I couldn't stop admiring in my hours of daydreaming.

"What do you want from us?" she said. "You were kind enough to escort my niece, and we thanked you for that profusely. But that's no reason to loiter in front of my house for all the neighbors to see. You think this is a bordello here or what?"

He blushed uncontrollably, and I was taken aback to discover that, sophisticated urbanite or not, my aunt could be quite crude when speaking to a man if she wanted to.

"No, really, let's be serious! You come and go, you're back and forth and hanging around. You show off and then what? This is a respectable home. You, a stevedore, you should

understand one thing: We don't need a man here. And certainly no hooligan!"

He stumbled for an instant then cried out abruptly:

"I've come to ask for the hand of the *bint el hassab wen nassab. . . .*"

"Bint el hassab wen nassab's hand is not available! So go, out with you, go away!"

"But I want to marry her according to the precepts of God and His Prophet."

"That's all fine and good, but I don't want that! Her parents have sent her here to rest, and now you're giving her a bad name, even though she doesn't know where Tangiers begins or ends."

He hesitated.

"I want to hear her say it!"

"You want to hear what?"

"I want to hear her say that she wants nothing to do with me. And stop shouting at me, or else I'll split your head in two with that pestle over there in the corner to your left, the one you put out to dry."

My aunt choked on her words. I fled to the kitchen, doubled up with laughter. The guy wasn't impressed by my aunt's haughty attitude, and that pleased me. When I came back to the patio, they were having a serious monosyllabic conversation. I felt redundant and went to the room that had become mine two weeks earlier, closing the door behind me. To distract myself, I counted the tiles that went from the bed to the

doorway and contemplated their resemblance to the brown diamonds that ran on a diagonal.

Dinner was short and quiet. I wondered how anyone could prepare fish and make it into a royal stew with just a few olives and some bits of preserved lemon. "This is a *marguet oumelleh*. A Tunisian neighbor gave me the recipe for the sauce," Aunt Selma said. "Remember the name and make sure that you always use grouper if you want it to be good. You know, your friend is quite touching. . . ."

I kept silent, soaking my taste buds with the fish sauce flavored with capers, retaining a mouthful of the tender white flesh.

"He is in love and he is sincere. He could make you happy. But I have the feeling that your ass isn't going to leave you alone. Oh, don't protest! You don't even know you have a cunt and that it can make the earth turn and cause the flowering almond trees to bow down and weep. You want to marry again?"

"No."

"No, because you don't know anything about men yet. Your Hmed skewered you, old goat that he is, but didn't go very far with his explorations. There's so much left to discover . . ."

"After what I've lived through, I am totally disgusted with men."

"Please, just be quiet for two seconds and listen to the old woman that I am, for 'the older the fiddle, the better the tune,'

as the proverb says. Who's talking about men? You haven't known men. Not at all. Now, I am sure that your stevedore of a Sadeq could light your fire. But he is penniless, and all he has are his tail and his heart with which to pray to God in heaven for some luck."

She lit a stick of incense, a cigarette, and with the pungent smell in her mouth, continued:

"If you want a man, a true man, and children as beautiful as the domes of Sidi Abdelkader, if you want to laugh all night and make your skin shine with jasmine balm without worrying about what tomorrow will bring, or whether you'll be rich one day dripping in gold and diamonds, all you have to do is take your stevedore. Right away. While you're still innocent and passionless. He loves you as only virgins can love."

For several minutes before she started up again, she paced up and down her room, or rather her alcove, in which everything was laid out lengthwise.

"But if you want something else . . . something better or much worse . . . if you'd like volcanoes and suns, if the earth isn't worth a dime in your eyes and you feel able to cut across it in a single stride, if you know how to swallow hot charcoal without groaning or walk on water without drowning, if you want a thousand lives rather than just one, to reign over entire worlds without being satisfied with any, well then Sadeq is not for you."

"Why are you talking to me this way? I don't want anything. You know that. I just want to forget and sleep."

50

"You'll sleep, but you'll ask yourself a thousand questions. At your age, troubles last as long as one tear wept, and joy is eternal, like your soul. All I'm asking you to do is to think it through and tell me tomorrow if you want this stevedore as a husband, yes or no."

I slept with my fists clenched, dreaming of no one, needing nothing. I didn't tell her anything the next day, more preoccupied with the fate of the geraniums than with my own, making sure that Adam, the completely wild tabby cat, would find his little meatballs at two in the morning so he could recover from his mating on the neighborhood rooftops.

Aunt Selma gave Sadeq permission to come whenever he wanted or could and sit on the olive-wood bench in the middle of the patio to talk and weep. Weep and talk. He told me that Tangiers was cruel, that he had escorted me right to the house of the lady who was said to be free, crazy, and beautiful enough to convert a demon to Islam. That he wanted me precisely because I never spoke to him and because I had eyes that kept him from sleeping. From working. From getting properly drunk on anisette with his buddies. That he came back to haunt the wharves of the Tangiers harbor when the mist rose and the ships wailed their sorrow, a cap on his head, his belly filled with steam, and his soul rent in two, shouting and cursing.

"If you leave me," he would say, "I'll go drift on the piers, and no lady who knows me will cry with joy when I come back, and no child will be sired by me. I beg you, Badra, don't let my mother be left without grandchildren."

He was an only child, and his mother lost her mind the day he threw himself under a freight train after I, dismayed and tired after a year of listening to his whimpering, told him:

"Go away, I really don't love you at all."

The Wedding Bath

They covered me in a veil from head to toe. I went through Imchouk's alleys surrounded by a swarm of cackling, simpering virgins. A whole horde of female cousins, relatives, and neighbors followed the procession, playing the tabla and ululating as befitted the event, my wedding bath.

When we arrived, clouds of disinfectant were already rising beneath the dome of the entrance hall. Alum stone and benjoin were burning in the braziers, and "Bismillahs" were flying from all sides like firecrackers. My new slip was a little tight underneath my armpits, and I was beginning to feel the need for air. Around me the virgins were pressing enormous white candles into the windowsills. Their dancing light told me that all of this was quite unreal.

Wrapped in a sheet that barely concealed her folds of fat, Neggafa stayed at my side, noisily and somewhat obscenely smacking gum. Dripping with sweat, I was in the middle of a crowd of half-naked women.

Then Neggafa made me lie down on a marble slab, and soon my skin was burning under the back-and-forth motion of her massage glove. She sprinkled me with warm water, covered me with ghassoul, *and began the actual massage. Her hands ran across my neck and shoulders, then over the full length of my back. In passing, they lifted my breasts and briefly kneaded them. It felt more than pleasurable. It was marvelous, in fact.*

The ghassoul, brown and scented, ran down my chest and dribbled toward my navel in a gentle hiss of popping bubbly. My nipples swelled, but Neggafa didn't seem to notice. She asked me to turn over on my belly, and then she spread my buttocks. My pubic bone hit the marble as her hands, unconcerned with my discomfort, pressed down on me. I felt a fireball crash down from the pit of my stomach to a spot between my thighs, and I panicked. But Neggafa's attention was elsewhere. I was her poultry to be plucked, her couscous pot. She was polishing and scrubbing me to earn her pay. A bucket of cold water roughly awakened me from a daydream of pleasure hard to own up to.

After the three ceremonial baths, it was time to remove any unwanted hair. That is when I thought I would die. My skin was scraped from my neck to my behind, but the henna ritual quickly made me forget my misery. Watching the virgins apply a little ball of the bride's henna to the center of their own palm

in the hope of being married as soon as possible reminded me of lambs dashing toward the slaughterhouse, with their fatty tails and innocent bleating. But I, too, was a lamb, meekly holding out my hands and feet to Neggafa, waiting to have my throat slit. My hands, wrapped in cotton and slipped into satin gloves, seemed cut off to me. Their saintliness was so pathetic. That night I dreamed of Neggafa's hands and prayed that Hmed's would at least be as gentle. And a bit bolder.

I came to love Tangiers, half Arab and half European, sly and calculating, singsong and God-fearing. I loved the fabrics laid out in the shop windows at the bazaars and never grew tired of watching Carmen, who was Spanish, cutting, measuring, and adjusting dresses, her mouth filled with pins, her varicose veins knotted and rigid like ropes. My aunt's seamstress was the taciturn sort. Sometimes, when we had our coffee break, she would speak about her son Ramiro, who had gone to Barcelona to seek his fortune, and her daughter Olga, who was getting ready to marry a Muslim. Her Arabic, mixed with Catalan patois, intrigued me. Yet I understood that she dreaded having to leave the land of her birth and die as an exile in Catalonia. She didn't have to experience that affront, however, and lived for a long time between her apartment on the boulevard in the modern city and the crowded Petit Socco, where her daughter had chosen to move. Her Muslim son-in-law paid for her funeral in the Christian district.

My aunt and I would go out dressed in the haïks that covered us from top to toe, and she would put on her *khama* Algerian style to be seductive.

"It's for ninnies to unveil themselves," she advised. "They don't know that they'll end up killing their men by depriving them of mystery." In the street, men would often turn around as we passed, praising the God who had made women so beautiful, the red of carnations so bright, and vegetable soup so fresh to the taste and smell. Each compliment left a sour flavor in my mouth and in the pit of my stomach.

Miniskirts were in style, and male students wore their hair long. The old radio broadcast the songs of Ouarda and Doukhali, and in the evening I went wild over the tales of Bzou, a comedian who made the whole country laugh into its farthest nooks and crannies. In Imchouk, too, I'm sure. One day, Aunt Selma gave me the news that Hmed had remarried. So he had repudiated me.

"Don't get excited too soon," she warned me. "Your brother Ali is still angry. He has sworn to purify the family honor by smearing yours across the streets of Tangiers."

"Because now he suddenly knows what honor is? Why didn't he think of that innocent girl's honor when he deflowered her under the eyes of Sidi Brahim!"

"You know perfectly well that the honor of cheap women isn't worth the paper it's written on. And you'd do better to take his threat seriously."

I tried but didn't manage to feel frightened. That was Tangiers's fault. The city had inoculated me with a delicious poison, and I was greedily drinking in its air, its whiteness, its freestone minarets, and its canopies. Women and starlings chirped in its patios. Their chatter put my mistrust of men to sleep. In this city, every gesture was elegant, every detail was important. And words, cloaked in sugar-sweet politeness, could become as cutting as shards of glass. Even scandal moved around on muffled feet, quickly grown stale, quickly stifled, its traces barely audible and almost never visible. Tangiers went to my head, and I loved its bubbles.

Aunt Selma was watching my metamorphosis from the corner of her eye, amused but determined to keep me from slipping and falling. Much later I understood that she had delivered Sadeq to me to keep my mind occupied and gain a few months of time before the volcano would erupt. Because she knew that sooner or later I would spew lava, and she was prepared for that. Just as she knew that Imchouk was burdened with a sleeping volcano held in reserve for the great carnival, so Slimane had declared to her.

I wasn't really surprised when she took in Latifa, a neighborhood orphan who was three months pregnant. In solidarity, the women around her had organized to remove the young girl from the inquisitive looks of the local shrews, sneaky and gossipmongering, and offer her shelter until after the delivery. I will always remember the little brunette who quietly shared our women's life, free inside and reserved in public, who

often went from laughter to tears without a warning. She helped with the housework and spent the afternoons embroidering miles of silk and linen, gratefully receiving the money from the sale of her fabric from Aunt Selma, her mother and friend. She gave birth one December night, assisted by the neighborhood midwife, who had been alerted to the first contractions that afternoon. The baby was received with a cautious ululation that must have pleased the cold flagstones in the courtyard and the sleeping lemon tree. Washed, anointed, and perfumed, he slept for three nights next to his mother's breast before a couple of childless cousins from the Rif adopted him. (Later on, he became one of the city's principal bankers.) Tangiers fell for the ruse, and Latifa was able to marry a modest waiter. Aunt Selma made sure the young woman would bleed copiously on her wedding night and never stopped blessing the God who had blinded men so that women could survive their cruelties.

My Brother Ali

Souad was not as lucky as Latifa. And my brother Ali is nothing more than a mule with pants on. Spoiled rotten, he never went to school and spent his time parading beneath the windows of important people in the hope of catching the eye of a silly but well-off little goose who would be seduced by his slicked-back locks and his pectorals hewn in granite. Souad, the daughter of the school principal, fell headlong into the trap and gave in to him in Sidi Brahim's mausoleum during the holy man's annual feast day. The family didn't find out about this until a year later. I had just left school, and Hmed was getting ready to ask for my hand.

Ali came to talk to my mother at her weaving loom one day. She jumped up as if a snake had bitten her. Distraught, she methodically began to flay her cheeks from her temples down to her chin. She wept silently for a long time. Her tears were the fine mist of a nameless catastrophe.

One month later, the principal's daughter crossed the threshold of our front door. She was sixteen—the same age as my brother. She was pregnant. The bloodstained blade of scandal had to be swallowed, and they needed to be married as quickly as possible.

Everything was done in a rush, and it started to look like a resounding fiasco. When the evening came, someone threw the girl's belongings in front of our door and disappeared into the night. Souad came into the clan with a dowry of three sheets, two pillowcases, and a cardboard box half-filled with dishes. My mother held it against her forever after.

"They forced her upon me, and I'll never forgive her for that," she would repeat over and over to her daughters and neighbors, forgetting that this "they" had a name, which was Ali, and that Souad was only a kid.

Souad understood the extent of her misfortune from the first night she spent under our roof. It made her lose her smile and then her voice. In silence, she helped my mother with the housework and the preparation of the family's food. It was clear from her white hands and her prematurely stooped back that she was used to being served rather than serving. She and Ali would pass without seeing or speaking to each other. She set his place at the table, put a napkin and a pitcher of

water there, and then retreated to the courtyard or kitchen. She slept in a tiny room, a poor little leper, spat upon and surrounded by hatred.

Her belly was growing, and she continued to focus on her navel with a vacant stare. She gave birth to a son, Mahmoud, had high fevers and hemorrhaged, and at the end of forty days chose to die.

Ali never dared take his child in his arms or kiss him. In spite of the hasty nuptials and the stamping of the marriage license, his son would always be a bastard, conceived outside the blessing of the clan.

Once the mourning period had passed, my mother forced Ali to marry one of our cousins.

"Only a woman of your own bloodline will be able to erase your shame and forget your past mistakes," she decreed sharply, visibly happy to have gotten rid of the intruder.

Ali did as he was told, in love with his mother and an obedient servant to the least of her wishes, both the most generous and the most depraved ones. Eventually, he began to resemble my father physically, growing taciturn and self-effacing, humble and satisfied. He joined the family workshop and helped his older brother get it back on its feet, wearing a woolen skullcap and a gray floor-length tunic. He grew a beard and

*let his muscles go slack. He went back to being nothing. Once
again he was a complete nobody.*

*Mahmoud, like his mother, never succeeded in being accepted
by the paternal tribe and disappeared when he was twelve.
They say he settled on the other side of the border in Malaga.*

Although we lacked nothing, I sensed that money was hard to come by and wondered how Aunt Selma managed to make ends meet. She embroidered exceptionally well but, by the end of the sixties, her clientele was decreasing and the young girls' trousseaux began to consist of modern items, imported from Europe or purchased on the spot in fashionable stores. Although Aunt Selma never complained of being responsible for me, I was embarrassed not to be able to contribute to the household expenses. She surmised as much, and one morning while she was cleaning vegetables for the evening meal, she cried out:

"God provides for the needs of birds and for the worms who live inside the stones! What are we to say about those people who curse Him all day long? It seems there is a crisis. I, on the other hand, claim we should follow our Algerian brothers' lead and collectivize everything! Yes, I heard it on the radio. Houari Boumedienne has requisitioned land and cattle to redistribute it fairly. If people don't want to share, they need to be hanged by their tongue that never utters the words *al hamdou lillah* enough!"

I soon discovered that my aunt, who was not averse to contradiction, was not content merely to be invited to evenings at the homes of the Tangiers bourgeoisie. She would also prepare the menu that the mistress of the house had stopped making, supervise the team of servants, oversee the pots of *harira* and the trays of tagine, and make sure that the *machroubat*, the flavored fresh beverages, were plentiful, as well. She started to make it a habit to take me along as kitchen help, recommending that I keep my eyes open and learn to conduct myself properly in society. For, once the meal was ready, she and I would change and mix with the fine company, where the people appreciated my aunt's caustic humor and her audacious ridiculing of all those who were full of themselves. Everyone knew she came from a good middle-class family and had been ruined by family inheritance quarrels and the rivalry of her sisters-in-law. Although a bit demoted, she was one of them.

I was never at ease at those parties. I always looked for a corner and sat there stiffly, my nerves on edge, trying not to be seen, too shy to speak, too proud to eat at the home of strangers. I would watch Aunt Selma circulating among the guests, complimenting this one, whispering something in confidence in the ear of another, her hand elegantly raising the hem of her richly embroidered caftan, and a radiant smile on her lips. Her stay in Imchouk had not spoiled either her teeth or her manners. The only thing she did bring back, unfortunately, was Bornia's hot-tempered spitting, not having had the heart to clean out her husband and thus protect herself from the vicissitudes of old age.

Uncle Slimane and Aunt Selma

The second great family scandal was caused by Uncle Slimane. Married to two women, he was the object of a double and fierce passion that brought his wives together rather than setting them against one another. He was neither handsome nor powerful; his jewelry store allowed him to live comfortably without being exorbitantly wealthy. He was stocky, with a small head, an overly large nose, and hair so rough that Selma would sometimes laughingly ask for a tuft of it to scrub her pots. But inside his saroual, *Uncle Slimane harbored an impressive member, and the wives discussed it between themselves, bright-eyed and with a half smile. Aunt Selma was not averse to boasting about her husband's unparalleled qualities as a lover, describing their frolicking in every detail to Bornia, the simpleton who, in exchange for a pound of meat or flour relayed them in a toned-down version to Imchouk's frustrated females.*

"He caresses her entire body. He licks her genitals, puts his tongue there and titillates its tip for a long time before

introducing his weapon. Selma gets skewered every night, from evening prayers until dawn. Now, there's a man for you! Not like those slowpokes you stuff full of lamb couscous and whey topped with fresh butter. Pfff!"

As long as Selma thought she was the sole proprietor of her husband's sex organ, her co-wife, Taos, not being very partial to his "thing"—so they said—everything went smoothly in her household. But the day she found out that Uncle Slimane was visiting the brothel, she turned into a raging tigress. War was declared, and Taos took her side:

"Never in our beds again!" they both decreed, irate allies, convinced of their right. My mother didn't know what to say, caught between wanting to laugh and fearing that this strike might make the rounds of the town and the farmers would snicker about it at night inside their shacks while riding their wives. As for Aunt Selma, she wasn't in the mood to laugh.

The village took sides with Slimane's legitimate wives against Farha and her two daughters, the whores of Imchouk. The adults were the only ones who knew that lightning had struck because of a roving cock. The women gave their men a cool reception. A hostile wind was rising, barring the mournful dicks' way to what lay carefully shaven between their legs.

Selma and Taos kept their word. Uncle Slimane came up against two locked doors instead of one and resigned himself to sleeping in the patio. His martyrdom lasted a week. He ranted and raved, threatened the strikers with a double repudiation, and ended up by giving in, sniveling his remorse, and swearing on the tomb of his father that he would never do that again. But there was a gaping rift, and Aunt Selma was deeply wounded.

"Slimane deceived not just his wife, but his beloved, the woman who loves him and who gave up everything for him," *she said to Bornia, who came to card wool a few days after the shearing had taken place. Sardonic and shamefully informal, the simpleton replied:*

"Why not just say it's your cunt pining for him?" Cut to the quick, Aunt Selma threw a ladle at her head that made a deep gash in her nose. Whimpering, Bornia left, giving her the finger.

Selma began to talk of Tangiers again, its cushy life, its bazaars, its proper toilets, treating Imchouk like a sewer of rats, and she increased the amount of salt in her stews—after taking away her gifts as a lover, depriving Slimane of her cooking talent next. Then one day she put on her haïk *and her high heels, crossed the patio, and slammed the door without so much*

as a glance for Slimane, who sat weeping and huddled beneath the pomegranate tree. The evening before, a bit theatrical but very much the grande dame, she had bared her chest and avowed to my mother:

"This is where he hurt me! This is where I'm bleeding!" I thought I was watching a wheat field burn in the middle of May.

It was not Aunt Selma who introduced me to Driss but a composer whose name I learned much later, Rimsky-Korsakov. The man who was to become my master and executioner was a brilliant cardiologist, a nervous and sophisticated thirty-something, recently returned from Paris. He would never have come to my attention had it not been for a sensual in-genue named Aïcha who sat down at the piano one evening at the house of a wealthy family in Marshan, one of the areas of Tangiers, and began to play *Scheherazade* by heart, so she said. I had never seen anyone play the piano—a huge crate taking up a quarter of the living room—and knew the names of symphonies even less. But I had been told I was to do my art apprenticeship in those circles that prided themselves on culture, preferably French.

Sunk back on a couch, surrounded by the kind of women who are half aristocrat, half call girl, Driss told daring jokes that made them burst with laughter, though they pretended to be shocked. Other dandies were standing around smoking, swaybacked, one with a rose, another with a carnation in his buttonhole,

streamlined mustaches curled up Ottoman-style. Some were thickset, with pudgy, hairy fingers. Many were smoking cigars.

Between two courses of fine pastries, Aunt Selma, who was going around with the trays, had a wink here or a discreet caress there for some of the guests. Each time her wine-colored caftan brushed against me, she'd whisper that so-and-so was the heir to immense properties in the Rif, another was the descendant of an important family of the Makhzen.

They were not all Andalusian or *Chorfa* or originally from Tangiers. I heaved a sigh of impatience as she came by again, which made her laugh:

"Open your eyes and ears," she murmured tenderly. "It will keep you from dying an idiot. And who knows, I may soon marry you off to one of these extravagant men with buckets of money," she added, severe and serious. I was not so sure of my flounced skirt or my shoes. Most of the women had exchanged their *babouches* and traditional attire for pumps and dresses that were tight fitting on top and flared below, whose fabric seemed both lavish and coarse at the same time. They all swayed their hips. I felt a little clumsy, very much the country girl, and it bothered me. Ill at ease, I was sweating from the top of my back to the bottom of my proper panties.

During one of those evenings, Driss forced my door open. I was in the kitchen gulping grenadine and fanning myself, wiping my neck and chest with a table napkin, when he suddenly burst in. He paused for a while, and then, when he saw

me rigid like a rabbit staring at headlights, he murmured, "My God, what a gem!"

"Excuse me, I came to look for ice cubes. I didn't mean to scare you."

"But . . ."

He opened the refrigerator, took a tray from the freezer, and began to loosen the ice cubes.

"Do you know where the lady of the house keeps her bowls?"

"No . . . I am a stranger!"

He turned around, laughing out loud.

"Me, too. I'm a stranger, also. You do have a name, I hope?"

"Badra."

"Ah, Badra, the moon! It causes hallucinations and migraines!"

He planted himself in front of me, the tray of ice cubes in his hands.

"My mother forbade me to sleep under the light of a full moon. Since I loved to disobey her, she was forced once a month to cover my skull with mashed squash and to collect my vomit in a bowl at the foot of the bed. It's a remedy that only she used. In any event, it's beautiful to make someone suffer so punctually!"

Nobody before Driss had ever uttered such outrageous remarks to me about our dear mothers.

He came toward me, and, terrorized, I pressed against the wall.

"Do I frighten you? With the name you have, it is I who should be fleeing!"

He left for the gigantic living room, lit by chandeliers heavy as sin, royal as the Versailles I was to see later on, without Driss and two steps ahead of Malik, my lover of the moment who was ten years younger than I.

Aunt Selma discovered me five minutes later in the same spot in the kitchen, petrified and pale.

"What's the matter with you? One would think you'd seen Azraël, the angel of death!"

"No, I'm all right. It's just too hot here!"

"Well, then, go to the garden for a while. You who so love flowers and scents, you'll be overwhelmed."

And I was. Never in my life had I seen such an opulence of plants, such an intemperance of flowers. Their perfumes wafted up, rich and distinct, fraternally linked to other scents whose name or precise structure I couldn't name. They were city plants that didn't grow in the country, intended for the pleasure of looking, while those at home were valuable only if we could consume them, sometimes nibbling them right in the fields like sheep. I became ecstatic over a hedge of white roses that seemed about to be set ablaze, hanging over a flower bed of wild mint and sage. I said to myself that the gardener must have been quite mad to combine so many contrasts.

Of course, that is where Driss flushed me out. That is where he took my icy hands in his. That is where he kissed my fingertips. I was trembling in the evening dew, wide-eyed and my

head feverish, when he turned my hands over to kiss their palms. He said nothing, and his lips were tender, warm, and light all at the same time. Without a trace of lechery. Everything was perfect: the sky above our heads, the immense silence like a protective womb, the held-in breath of the night. Why did he do this to me?

Of course I felt like crying. Of course I wouldn't let myself.

He raised his head, held my fingers for thirty seconds, then left in his white suit, his footsteps crunching the gravel of a path as long as my life that had only just begun. When he stepped across the threshold of the large French doors of the living room, I began to grow old. Inexorably.

I stayed in the garden for a long time. Alone. Without a body. Without husband. Without children. I heard Rimsky-Korsakov being played again, dark and sweet, by Driss's fingers. Aunt Selma told me the composer's name later when we had gone home and were alone like two widows. At least, that was the impression I had. She was in a hurry to dispose of my questions, telling me that staying up late was never good for the complexion.

Much later, Driss told me about Rimsky-Korsakov and put a name to the notes that Tangiers had absentmindedly delivered to me between two doors. I had just met the man who was to rend my heaven in two and give me my own body like the quarter of an orange. He who had "visited" me as a child, Driss, had come back to me. Driss had been reincarnated.

Badra's Childhood

I met him when I was very small, near the bridge that goes over the Harrath Wadi, one silent night without stars. I had barely begun to go across when a hand grasped my shoulder. It was very dark, and the wadi was exhaling its vapors, a flow of hot water in a stony, ice-cold landscape. Even the rocks seemed to have stopped breathing. I said to myself, "Here we go. You'll finally see that malevolent spirit, the great Efrit with his cloven hooves. He'll drink your soul and throw you in the wadi. Your mother won't call your name again and will never see your body anymore." But the hand let go of my shoulder, caressed my throat, and then tenderly pressed down on my breasts. My "fava beans," as they call budding breasts in Imchouk, must not have been enough for that hand, for it fiddled with my behind for a moment before snapping the elastic of my little girl's panties. Then it clung to my sex organ, hairless and closed.

Feverish fingers wandered inside the furrow in the center, and their touch was rather friendly. I closed my eyes, trusting

and consenting. One finger freed itself and ventured to an unfamiliar spot. I felt a slight burning, but instead of closing my thighs, I opened them more. I thought I heard the wadi sigh and then burst out laughing.

Then the hand withdrew, and I sunk to the glazed grass. The sky began to shimmer again, and the frogs started their concert anew. A second heart had been born between my legs, and it was beating after a hundred years of stupor.

"So you maintain that I appeared to you that night in Imchouk, near the wadi, and that it was I who revealed your secret garden to you in a few beats and three caresses?" Driss concluded, his head on my navel, his hands wandering up and down my thighs, a century after the Annunciation. "And why not, after all? Sooner or later everyone receives a sign that tells him about his fate. But am I truly yours, my gentle apricot? Ibliss, that liar devil, loves to cloud the issue and misrepresent the truth."

It's odd that Driss spoke of Satan that day as a comment on my confidences. It was all well and good that I knew he was teasing me, but a slight sense of uneasiness crept into my mind. I had experienced a moment of light. And if the messenger of my childhood was not an angel, it was certainly not a demon, either. Or else, it was neither one nor the other but simply a man. And he was mine.

It had been a few months since a dike had cracked inside my head, and my anger was rising like a tidal wave. I held it against Imchouk that it had connected my genitals with evil, had forbidden me to run, to climb trees, or to sit with my legs spread. I held it against those mothers who watch the girls, check their gait, palpate their lower abdomen, and eavesdrop on the sound they make when they take a piss to be sure their hymen is intact. I held it against my mother that she had all but armored my genitals and had married me off to Hmed. I held it against ravens, toads, and dogs that they were carrion eaters. I held it against myself that I had left school for a husband and had said nothing when Neggafa put her finger in

my cunt, just to check that I was a true dimwit who accepted dying too soon.

And that's the story. I told myself that I was not a tattle-tale. That I wanted to close my eyes, go to sleep, die, and be resuscitated by drums and trumpets and have Driss in my arms. Since the Annunciation on the bank of the wadi, I knew what I wanted—to watch the sun without blinking, to the point of losing my eyesight. I had my sun between my legs. How could I have forgotten that?

Badra's Almond

Back home I put my head under the blankets, pulled down my panties, and looked at the little smooth and round triangle that had received the homage of an unfamiliar hand but one I knew to be a loving one. I took the same course again with a dreamy index finger. With eyelids closed and quivering nostrils, I swore that one day I would have the most beautiful sex in the world and it would impose its laws on men and stars, pitiless and relentless. The only thing was that I didn't know what such an object might look like once it had gained maturity. Suddenly I was afraid that one of the women in Imchouk would have one just as beautiful, be able to compete with mine, and reduce my oath to ashes. I wanted to be sure that where genitals were concerned the world would have no others to adore.

I decided to watch the women, to be on the lookout for an appearance of their private jewel to know which model might rival mine in beauty and power. It wasn't easy for me to flush it out. Neither my mother nor my sister ever undressed in front

of me. And although I sometimes found traces of caramelized sugar on the floor or in the sink, I never caught them in the act of removing their hair. In the hammam, women wrap themselves in the three yards of their pagne *or keep their* saroual *on, and when they are ready to rinse off, they hide behind a door and only come out with towels around their body, draped and glistening like statues. Women are never naked in front of little girls for fear of definitively assaulting the innocence of their gaze and compromising their status as a future bride.*

The summer gave me a chance to satisfy some of my curiosity. Farm women filled up the patios and terraces to help the affluent put up couscous, hot peppers, tomatoes, caraway, and coriander for the winter. Nomadic women, too, with their piercing look and rough patois, joined in this laborious and homespun task, reading coffee dregs and selling amulets. Beggar women were content just to tap on doors and hold out their hands, sure they would receive some wheat or a chunk of dried mutton.

I spent the brightest afternoons with Aunt Selma and her co-wife, Taos, on the western bank of the village. The flames of the bread oven would sputter throughout the day. Peppers, corn on the cob, and benzoin were roasting on the grill. The abundance brought solace to the heart and made it want to give its riches away without counting.

The house had two floors, each with four rooms. Selma would move from one to the other under the gentle gaze of Taos, her accomplice. It was no secret to anyone that the latter was just as attached to the woman from Tangiers as Slimane himself was. It was she who had gone to the city for the first time in her life to ask for her rival's hand in marriage on behalf of her husband. "You're crazy!" her family and neighbors had exclaimed. "She is younger than you, and she's a city girl. You're going to bring a viper into your home who is bound to bite you." "I know what's good for my own home," Taos had answered. That is how, against all traditions, Selma's father had nothing to do with Slimane's brothers and uncles but dealt instead with Taos, who, respectful of the proprieties, formulated the request for marriage standing behind a curtain.

Once a week, Spanish women, with the same severe swishing of their flouncing black skirts and the rustling noise of their wicker baskets filled with silk and tiny silver and lace items, would knock on the door of the two wives. Inquisitive and nosy, their heads uncovered and in bare feet, farm women would follow. In contrast to the women of means, they were allowed to go unveiled without risking disapproval.

Seeing the patio crammed full, the women laughing together, and the workers busy with the intense labor of summer, was pure bliss. I wasn't forgetting my oath of examining everything

to find out more. But the wool carders kept their legs stubbornly crossed. Those who washed the blankets in their hitched-up dresses would reveal just their calves, and those busy stuffing mattresses did raise their heavy rumps but kept them jealously hidden from any indiscreet looks.

Only the farm women rolling the grains of couscous could help me explore their secret, for they would sit with their legs spread wide around enormous wooden basins in which they mixed water and semolina. I would pretend to observe the movement of their hands and sieves but focused my attention on Bornia, the simpleton. Her obesity forced her to be constantly moving, her buttocks scraping the ground, and sweating copiously. Known for her crude language and her obscene gestures, the farm girl would raise the bottom of her dress every two minutes and fan herself. I was on the lookout for a revelation. It wasn't forthcoming. And Bornia, nasty as could be, blurted, "What are you staring at me like that for? Go on with you, play somewhere else or I'll show you what hell is!"

Bornia didn't know that was exactly what I wanted. To see her grown-up private parts so I could compare. I bolted without asking any questions.

Since little girls were forbidden to be present at women's conversations, I learned how to become part of the scenery and have them forget about me. I saw Aunt Selma's cronies and

servants whisper, then burst out laughing, bend to each other, touch their breasts or belly, and compare their jewelry and tattoos. Sometimes Bornia was inspired. She would stand up and make some vague motions with her pelvis that would unleash hysterical laughter from the group. On occasion, the wife of Aziz the shepherd would take over. Armed with a carrot, she would stick the big stalk between her thighs and do a bawdy dance, moving the carrot up and down and from right to left, swaying lewdly. Mothers and wives laughed, slapped their thighs or chests or, scandalized, covered their mouth or eyes.

"*Stop that! You'll end up thinking it's real if you keep that up,*" *a neighbor shrieked.*

"*Let her be!*" *another protested. "Aziz must have a shriveled one and she's making up for it with whatever comes her way!*"

Out of breath, the dancer answered:

"*What he has, the scoundrel, is not a carrot but an ax handle. When he enters me, I feel like I'm being skewered by the bull's horn.*"

"*What bull is that?*"

"*The one who carries the earth on his head so it won't fall down on your heads, you sinners!*"

The group would laugh wildly.

"*And you, Farida?*" *Aunt Selma asked.*

The imam's daughter would answer:

"When it's resting, it bounces and gleams like a half moon. When it's hard, it is the sword of an Islamic warrior. I resist only to arouse greater assaults."

"Does he whisper things in your ear?"

"No, he brays like Chouikh's donkey! Sometimes I think he's gone mad, that's how much he groans when he comes!"

"No way," Selma interrupted, teasing her. "It's your treasure trove that's making him crazy."

"Speaking of which," the imam's daughter would retort, "you, city girl, you should give us the recipe. What do you do in the city to keep your pussy white as ivory?"

"There's nothing easier, but I'm not going to tell you. You have to be insane to reveal your magic tricks to another woman."

"At least tell me what to do to shrink my vagina. Kaddour claims he feels nothing when he takes me because the entryway is so big and he can't reach the back."

"I won't tell you anything, you pack of females in heat! I only share my secrets with my dear friend Taos!"

Squinting her eyes with a malicious smile, Taos answered:

"Do what she does! Go to the baths more often! That's her secret, just plain water. That's what gives her that peachy complexion and that European skin!"

"It's true," Aunt Selma retorted. "Water is woman's first perfume and her best beauty cream. After that, just to answer you, you faithless bunch, you should make sure you keep your private parts fresh and smooth. Groom them with a cloth moistened with lavender and perfume their edges with musk or amber. Nothing should repel your man, not their smell or their touch. He should feel like biting them before stuffing anything else in there."

"He's never even looked at them," the shoemaker's wife complained, "so there's no point in talking about biting or kissing them!"

"A good thing, too," the imam's daughter whispered. "He'd end up blind if he did!"

"The one who holds the grace of God in his hands without knowing how to pay it homage is the one who's blind," Aunt Selma concluded.

What I am left with of those warm and aromatic afternoons is the laughter of cloistered women and the nostalgia for harvests. What I miss, too, are the bits of news and the gossip. Who is the most recent wife to have been repudiated in the village? What has become of the two epileptics? Who has the biggest cock these days, and who has been made a cuckold by his shepherd? Are they still exchanging recipes for overcoming perspiration, remedying bad breath, periods that are too heavy, vaginas that are too dry or too wet, pubic hair that grows sideways and causes infections? Could Imchouk have sold its secrets to urban doctors and charlatans? Has it resigned itself to do as other people do, confiding its paltry miseries to the notoriety of the tabloids? I wouldn't know. I don't read newspapers in Tangiers. Out of respect for Driss.

In the end, no adult female private parts ever deigned to show themselves to my childhood eyes. Fortunately, there were the eyes of Moha the potter to console me. Sitting in front of his stall, he would look me over from top to bottom with open greed every time I passed by. No matter how I rushed on, respecting the instructions that prohibited Imchouk's virgins from speaking with the potter at all, his ogling of my lower half gave me shivers and an obscure desire. Moha was partial to little girls and especially those who, like me, had a beauty mark on their chin.

Chouikh, who sold fritters, loved kissing my knee when it bled. As soon as he saw me, he'd leave his stall, where a huge pot of boiling oil was smoking away, lift me up to the ceiling, and cry out to the first passerby, "God preserve us from this little one when she's all grown up. She's going to flow like a fountain of honey in this godforsaken place of thorns!" Then he'd kiss the back of my knee and give me two fritters as tawny as his hair.

I was proud of having two courtiers whose stares attracted me like a magnet. Something told me I had them in the palm of my hand and would be able to do with them whatever I wanted. But what? My power was inevitably linked to my mouth, my beauty mark, the shape of my legs, and even more surely to my private parts. To be convinced of that, I only needed to see my father eye my mother's rump or hear Uncle Slimane beg Lalla Selma to give him her gum to chew, which was scented with her saliva.

I knew that the eye of the storm lay hidden inside my genitals, but what I didn't know yet was whether I was a sandstorm, a snowstorm, or a hailstorm. I was merely afraid that I would die without having exploded in Imchouk's sky.

Driss did not rape or assault me. He waited for me to come to him, in love, with my feet caught in my hair like the Hilalian Jazia, virginal and new, speechless and without any hope. He waited until I surrendered myself to him, and that, against all better knowledge, is what I did. Against the good advice of Aunt Selma, who, seeing right through me, would not calm down.

"You're a complete idiot! Driss is rolling in dough and adores frightened little deer like you. And you can find nothing better to do than to fall in love with him! What you need to do is get married, you poor dope. Where do you think you're living? You're in Tangiers, and your father, may God rest his soul, was nothing but a poor tailor of djellabas."

I just fanned the brazier, keeping the fire going, on which was simmering a lemon tajine whose smell wafted into the farthest crannies of the house. I could only have respect for Aunt Selma, a woman who stubbornly cooked on a wood fire when Tangiers was already discussing stoves and bringing them back from Spain to show off. She had the reputation

of being a first-class chef, and her meatballs as well as her fish stews made all the mouths of Tangiers water. Standing beside her in the dark kitchen of the rue de la Vérité, I closely watched her gestures and her herb containers, dreaming of grasping the secret of her recipes. I wanted to cook the way she did and make Tangiers weep in ecstasy, as the singer Abdelwahab was to make me weep much later beneath the dome of heaven, alone in the fields, free and cleansed of all desire. Almost at peace.

Driss had done some investigating. He knew I had been married. He didn't breathe a word of this and took six months to pluck me. He gave me time to fantasize about his voice, his hands, and his smell. He let me ripen quietly during long pomegranate-filled afternoon naps.

We saw each other several times at fancy evenings without ever touching, without exchanging any looks or a hello that was anything but neutral and distant. He came to have lunch twenty times at my aunt's house. Not a single improper word or inappropriate gesture. Later I understood that it was a snake dance. Neither Driss nor Aunt Selma looked into the other's eyes, but they both knew he was out for the kill. He wanted me. She, on the other hand, was defending my entryway, a sacred cobra standing guard in front of my body, which was dying to come alive but which I knew so little, and which she judiciously wanted to turn into cash to make sure I would live a comfortable life as a woman of independent means.

I was a disappointment to her, and she never again came rushing to soothe my female wounds. I also know that she felt contempt for me. Many years later, when no one thought to ask forgiveness of one's own tears anymore, I had to admit she was right.

At the time, however, I was somewhere else, besotted with love and sentimentalism. I would bite my lips to make them redder and hum little Egyptian melodies to give an impression of composure when Driss came to the house, for he would announce each upcoming visit to my aunt via a porter. Usually, the porter arrived around nine o'clock in the morning, loaded down with two heavy baskets filled with fruit and vegetables. I would always find a package of *swak*, henna, pomegranate bark, and a vial of kohl. Late in the afternoon, when Driss, having had his fill of tajine and various pastries, would leave for the city and his appointments, my aunt made a mixture of his henna with water, the smell of which used to give me a migraine. On the large patio, she and the swallows that had returned to the fold would chirp in unison, disconnected from the rest of the world and quenched by an unknown source. The birds would go back to their nests and their mates, while my aunt would wash and massage herself, remove unwanted hair, enhance herself with dry perfumes and somewhat suggestive henna patterns, just above her left breast, for example, and then, eccentric and alone, withdraw to her large bedroom full of nail-studded trunks and mottled mirrors

without asking me if I felt lonely. I learned later on that she had an invisible lover. A genie from another world. It used to bewilder me, but I endorsed her right to be free without ever wanting to know further details. I just wanted her to be happy.

Driss got me settled in his living room, gave me strawberries and blueberries. Then he ran a bath, carried me at arm's length, and sat me fully dressed in the bathtub, its water fragrant with orange blossoms. Chopin whirled between the walls of the house, and through the collar of Driss's shirt I glimpsed his dense black hair.

He took my shoes off, caressed my toes and the bottoms of my feet. I was frozen. His mouth and breath burned my neck, ran down the full length of my legs. My breasts engorged and the wet fabric that was clinging to my skin made the nipples stand out, making me even more naked under his watchful eye. He squeezed and nibbled on them, and they doubled in size between his teeth. I was trembling, terrified, like a bird caught in a tornado, my womb aching with desire, my belly contracted with terror. What was he going to do to me? What had I come looking for?

He undressed me slowly, delicately, the way you loosen the fragile skin from a green almond. In the steam of the bathroom, I could barely distinguish his features. Only his eyes,

which bored into me, drilling my heart and my vagina, masters of my fate. I told myself I was a whore. But I knew that I was not. Unless it was like the pagan goddesses of Imchouk, who were uninhibited femmes fatales, stark raving mad.

He soaped my upper and lower back, covered my pubis with foam. Its hair concealed my privacy from his look, but his fingers quickly slid beneath my panties and opened the lips, finding my clitoris, hard as a chickpea, then pressed down with a delicate and meditative gesture. I moaned, tried to take down my panties, but he wouldn't let me. He turned me over, embraced my thighs, and made me arch my back. There you are, I said to myself. You are his plaything. His object. He can do anything now, rip out your tongue, tear open your heart, or make you the Queen of Sheba.

Lowering my panties, he put his cheek on my buttocks, spreading the crack with his fingers and making room for his nose. I was wet. Then he took a small flask from one of the shelves, removed a drop of oil, and perfumed my anus with it, massaging it for a long time, to the point that I forgot my trepidation and my muscles began to relax as his knowledgeable hands became more focused. I had no idea what he wanted to do to me but was wishing that he would just do it and certainly not stop the circular motion that was driving me wild, opening me up for him, as my vagina discharged its joy in long translucent strands.

He found the spot, reaped my wetness, and daubed my buttocks with it before sinking his teeth in. No bite has ever

been dearer to me. I could hear my belly laugh, weep, then bubble over with excitement. I begged, "Enough . . . enough," praying all the while that he wouldn't stop.

Then he carried me, dripping wet and moaning, to the bed. As soon as he bent over to lay me down, I pulled him by the collar, put my mouth on his, sucking his tongue, making the buttons on his shirt pop open, and bit his torso. He was laughing, beaming, squeezing my breasts with both hands, drawing their incandescent tips into his mouth, one finger roaming the edge of my soaking entry. My patience exhausted, I managed to inhale the dawdling visitor. My orgasm threw me up against him, panting and deeply embarrassed.

He didn't give me any time to catch my breath, guided my hands toward his fly and watched me open it. Incredulous, I discovered a sex organ that was stronger and larger than those I had seen before. It was brown and ripe, its skin silky and its glans impressive. I put my lips on it, improvising a caress until then unknown to me. He let me do it and watched me almost faint. I had him in my mouth and the magic of that touch alone made my belly convulse. I had no idea what animal was churning around inside there, nor why this cock provided me with so much pleasure as it came and went between my lips, rubbing my palate, gently tapping my teeth as it moved by. Driss remained upright, eyes closed, his flat belly filling me with the amber smell of his sweat and skin.

He left my mouth, raised my legs. The head of his penis knocked against my vagina. I pushed to help and let him in,

but a hideous burning bowled me over. He took up the charge again, tried to interfere, ran into an unforeseen tightness, withdrew, and wanted to force the passage. I was moaning but not with pleasure anymore, now with pain, still wet but incapable of letting him enter. He took my face in his hands, licked my lips, then said smitten and laughing:

"My word, you're a virgin!"

"I don't know what's happening to me."

"What's happening to you is what happens to any woman when she neglects her body for too long."

He realized that I was in pain, caressed my back, licking and nibbling, sucking at my labia for a long time. He never lost his hardness for a moment, his cock feverishly striking against my belly, my buttocks, and my legs.

It was only when he supported my back with a pillow, placed his sex at the entrance of my rosebud, insisting on slipping in a few millimeters at a time, that he was finally able to fill me up, dilating my dripping wet walls, massaging my womb, pounding me with long slow movements, his sweat dripping on my breasts. He managed to open me, possess me, widen me until I was breathless, smoothing my lungs and the tiny fibers of my belly. His sperm gushed out in long streams and, like rain, flowed against my exposed wetness, purifying its earlier debasement.

He remained snuggled against me for a long time, and it was only when he was groping for his packet of cigarettes that I saw his tears.

He didn't want me to get dressed again or put my wet panties on; he just smiled when he saw me hide my private parts with my hands. I sensed his bafflement, caused as much by my modesty as my awkwardness. Eyes half closed, he muttered, "Ah, if only you could see yourself!" I was afraid he might dislike some detail of my body. He guessed that, held my arms behind my back, drank from my mouth, then put his head between my legs. I shrank back, bruised with pleasure and pain. My second deflowering had made me unable to tolerate any further caress.

"Don't go home tonight, Badra, my wounded kitten," he asked.

"Aunt Selma won't sleep a wink all night."

"I'll deal with her tomorrow. In the meantime, look what I have for you."

He took a midnight blue box from the inside pocket of his jacket. Two diamonds lay sleeping inside it. Two limpid drops of water. I gave him back the opened box.

"What are you doing?"

I kept silent, tormented by too many contradictory feelings.

"They've been waiting for you for a month. I didn't know how to give them to you without offending you."

He took my hands in his, as he had done the first evening, and skimmed across them with a kiss.

"I've been waiting for you for so long, Badra."

I looked at him, dying to believe him, but mistrusting the man after being showered with the male of him.

"You're a *houri*, you know? Only houris recover their virginity after every coitus."

I answered in cold and almost sarcastic anger:

"You're like all the others! You want to be the first!"

"But I am the first! And I don't give a damn about the others and what they want. I want you, you, my almond, my butterfly!"

He attached the water drops to my ears, caressing the lobe of each with the tip of his tongue. As if in a flash of lightning, I became aware that he was completely naked and that his cock had not grown slack. Worse, I discovered that I was still hungry and thirsty for his kisses and his sperm.

Desire is contagious, and Driss was very astute. He forced my legs open, smoothed my crumpled flesh, and applied a balm to soothe my irritated spots. Then he slipped his sex between my breasts and pressed them together, half serious, half playful.

"Every particle of your skin is a bed of love and a source of ecstasy," he said.

I blushed, remembering the power he had used to explore my every nook and cranny. But I couldn't feel guilty, disparaged, or outraged. His cock came and went between my breasts, gently bumping against my mouth at the end of each motion. When he flooded my chest with his milk, I sighed, sated. He delicately spread his liquid on my throat, put a finger to my lips to have me taste it. Driss was sweet and salty.

I shivered when he whispered in my ear:

"You'll see, one day you'll drink me! When you feel completely confident."

I felt like answering him, "Never," but remembered the pleasure he had just given me. The taste of eternity. The world had suddenly become a caress. The world had become a kiss. And I was nothing but a floating lotus flower.

The following day it was not only I who was in love with Driss. My genitals, too, revered him.

Happiness? Happiness is making love because of love. It's when the heart threatens to explode because it's beating, when an incomparable look lingers on your mouth, when a hand leaves a bit of its sweat in the hollow of your left knee. It's the saliva of the beloved that flows down your throat, sweet as sugar and transparent. It's your neck stretching out, letting go of its knots and fatigue, becoming endless because a tongue is running up and down its full length. It's your earlobe pulsating like your lower belly. It's your back becoming delirious and inventing sounds and shivers to say I love you. It's the raised leg, consenting, the panties falling down like a leaf, useless and bothersome. It's a hand penetrating the forest of hair, awakening the roots of the head and generously watering them with its tenderness. It's the terror of having to open up and the incredible power of giving yourself when everything in the world is a reason to weep. Happiness is Driss, hard inside me for the first time, his tears dripping into the hollow of my shoulder. Happiness was he. Happiness was I.

The rest was merely common graves and garbage dumps.

The Night of Deflowering

The party was over, and I was ready to leave, giving up any hope of going back to my parental home. I leaned over to my mother and, as tradition requires, muttered, "Please forgive me for the pain I have caused you."

The formula sealed the separation. My brother bent down to take off my shoes. He put a little money in one of them, then carried me outside. The donkey belonging to Naïma's father-in-law was waiting to take me to my new family's house, just five hundred yards away.

"I need a kid! Quickly!" Chouikh, the fritter vendor, cried out.

A little boy was to accompany me during the short trip to bring me luck. "I want Mahmoud, my nephew," I murmured. Choosing a bastard, a bad luck omen, to make destiny contrite so it would grant me male children showed some nerve. I got what I wanted and hugged Ali's son close to me openly and publicly before the incensed females.

Uncle Slimane was holding the reins and advanced with stooped back and his turban undone. One mule leading another, and Aunt Selma was far away.

My mother-in-law was waiting for me, her three daughters by her side. Their ululations were too high-pitched, and the almonds they threw as a sign of welcome seemed like stones. Slimane picked me up by my waist and set me down in front of the witches' hedge.

Neggafa and Naïma escorted me to the nuptial bedroom. My sister insisted on undressing me, to the annoyance of Neggafa, whose charge this really was. She unhooked my dress in silence, and I whispered:

"What's going to happen now?"

Without looking up, she answered in the same whisper:

"The same thing that happened between my husband and me the night you slept at our house, in our bedroom. Now you know."

So she knew that I knew. Neggafa began to recite her instructions:

"As soon as we leave, you will shake your shoe in front of the door seven times and say, 'May God make my husband love me and not look at any other woman but me.'"

She fumbled in her blouse and took out a sachet:

"Put this powder in the glass of tea I've placed on the table. Make sure your husband takes a few sips of it."

But she wasn't able to hand me the sachet, as my mother-in-law burst into the room without a warning, holding a brazier in her hand emitting thick clouds of incense.

"My son will be here soon!" she shouted. "Hurry up!"

Naïma took off my bra and then my panties. I felt like laughing out loud—as soon as it was sure of its rights and its straight and narrow path, my decent little village could be so obscene.

Before handing me over to Hmed, Neggafa murmured in my ear:

"Put your shirt beneath your buttocks, so it will absorb the blood. It's cotton, and the stains will be quite visible."

Suddenly severe, she then added:

"Don't let him leave his seed inside you. Your vagina will be too wet, and men don't like that. Lie down on the bed. He'll be here very soon."

It was my sister's turn; she leaned over to me:

"Close your eyes, bite your lips, and think about something else. You won't feel a thing."

Then I was alone, my wedding dress like a sheepskin at the foot of the bed. I stood in front of the mirror of the huge armoire and looked at myself, completely naked! My skin was gleaming in the candlelight, smooth and hairless. My hair fell down my back in waves, and the henna patterns on my arms filled the air with fragrance. My breasts stood up, firm and proud. I covered

them with my hands. What were they going to be subjected to, what would they discover? There were so many stories about the wedding night and its tortures. So many scandals as well.

My cousin Saïd had been the laughingstock of every cottage all the way to Algeria. The good man who, as a boy, had once made me show my private parts to his little buddies had not been able to confront his wife's and turned out to be a true virgin. He wanted to flee, to the despair of his family and friends.

"Are you a man or not?" one of them had exclaimed, beside himself.

"Take it easy. I'll get there, but there's no point in roughing me up!"

"You make people beg you to skewer a woman?"

"Give me some time to breathe!"

Then, from the back of the courtyard, his father thundered in a rage:

"Fine, you go there now or I'll go in your place!"

Saïd went but wasn't able to deflower Noura, his wife. His mother declared that he had been bewitched. She went into the couple's bedroom, undressed, and ordered her son to pass between her legs seven times. The remedy must have worked, because Saïd immediately found his virility and was able to deflower Noura with much blood and shrieking.

I shivered. I lay down on the bed and pulled the covers up, naked and forsaken by everyone.

When I opened my eyes again, I saw Hmed standing before me. It was the third time we'd met after the engagement and the Eid celebration, when he had come to bring the gift of the moussem. *I don't know whether it was fatigue or emotion, but he seemed older than I remembered. He sat down on the edge of the bed, looked at me, then passed a timid hand over my neck and breasts. He muttered, "Now there's a royal piece!"*

He took off his shoes, spread a rug on the floor, and prostrated himself twice. Then he joined me in the bed.

All I could see was his torso and his arms covered with white hair. He shoved a pillow under my lower back and roughly pulled me toward him. His lower lip was trembling and humid. I had my nightshirt under my buttocks and Hmed on my chest. He spread my legs, and his penis banged against my vagina. Bornia was laughing in the fields, the stumps of her teeth frightening the carrots. The sex organ groping between my legs was blind and dumb. It hurt me, and with every one of its movements I tightened up a little more. The audience was pounding on the door, demanding to see my virgin's shirt. I tried to extricate myself, but Hmed had me nailed down beneath his weight and, penis in hand, attempted to push it in. No success. Sweating and breathing hard, he lay me down on the sheepskin, raised my legs

at the risk of dislocating my joints, and began the attack again. My lips were bleeding, and my lower belly was on fire. Suddenly I wondered who this man was. What was he doing there, toiling above me, messing up my hair, and causing my henna's arabesques to fade with his putrid breath?

At last he let go of me and jumped up. His lower body wrapped in a towel, he opened the door and called his mother. She stuck her head inside right away, Naïma hot on her heels.

"Oh!" my sister cried out.

I don't know what she saw, but it couldn't have been a pretty sight. My mother-in-law was fuming with rage, seeing that the wedding night was turning into a fiasco.

On her own authority, she spread my legs and then yelled:

"She's intact! Fine. We have no choice! We have to tie her down!"

"Please, I beg you, don't do that! Wait! I think she's mtaqfa. *My mother armored her when she was little, and she forgot to undo the protection."*

They were talking about a ritual as old as Imchouk itself, which consists of padlocking the hymen of small girls with magical formulas, making them impregnable even to their husbands unless they are unlocked by a contrasting ritual. All I knew was that Hmed was revolting to my body, which is why it forbade him access.

My mother-in-law tied my arms to the bars of the bed with her shawl, and Naïma took it upon herself to hold down my legs. Terrified, I realized that my husband was going to deflower me under the eyes of my sister. With one hard blow, he broke me in two, and for the first and only time in my life, I fainted.

The trophy of my maidenhead was passed from hand to hand. From mother-in-law to aunts via the neighbors. Old women daubed their eyes with it, convinced that it prevents blindness. The bloodstained shirt proved nothing except the stupidity of men and the cruelty of submissive women.

One thing was certain: Hmed was going to make love to a corpse for the five years of our ghastly marriage.

How many times did I go back to Driss's mouth that night when I ran away from Aunt Selma's house for the first time? Twenty, thirty times? All I know is that I lost my virginity there. The real one. The virginity of the heart. Since then, my soul has merely been a station platform where I stand to watch men fall.

At first, I didn't want him to put his tongue inside my vagina, shocked by his shamelessness. But in the few atoms of a second when his lips brushed my mound, I felt the universe topple, seas overflow, and planets implode. Lightning cracked my body and my head, setting fire to everything I had experienced until that instant. I didn't know that a caress could have such intensity, that a man could give me such pleasure.

Because Driss put his tongue in my vagina, I decided to remove the hair from it. To see my nudity before seeing him again. I wanted to know what it looked like exactly, that animal that had so disgracefully drooled its desire for Driss, sheltered by its curly, teasing hair, ready to do anything to welcome that expert and laughing mouth back again inside its sheath

and experience once more the wild pleasure enjoyed the day before.

It was a tough business. You had to carefully supervise the caramelized sugar, work it for a long time so it would become soft without liquefying. Removing the hair from your pussy is not the same as shaving your legs or armpits. I was afraid to confront the dense mop that had lain quietly and secretly sleeping between my thighs ever since my marriage, the time my husband had taken me like the leg of a chair pushed into a rug, self-centeredly, and without knowing anything about my different recesses or my desires, which I discovered were blazing and rebellious.

The pain is horrible when the caramel is plastered against the skin. I hate physical suffering. Valiantly, I spread the wax on the large labia and discovered to my astonishment that there was hair growing inside the surface as well, where the hidden flesh is soft and shining. One application of wax, then two. The pain passed quickly and was followed by pleasure, that traitor. How? I don't know. Instead of contracting and shriveling, the flesh gleamed, opened wide, and the vagina's opening became moist. The wax coating slides, finds nothing to hold on to. Flesh turns into seawater, offering no grasp. The ball becomes fragrant with my juice at every passage. My genitals, I notice, are enjoying this, having their hair pulled out, being martyred. Desire detonates my head. I become an accomplice with this unknown flesh, capricious and imperious. I was afraid of hurting myself, and here I am, my cunt in delight and wide awake.

The creased small labia are pounding beneath my hand, sticky with wax. I am ready to faint. Under the flow of warm water that is loosening a few lumps of sugar sticking to the skin, I am looking at a well-developed, silky vagina, resembling the one I discovered under the covers when I was little, but now full and ripe like a fruit. Cautiously, then more and more eagerly, I explore it again, wearing its crown of devilish and superb virginity. It wants more. I have neither Driss nor Bornia's carrot at hand. I take hold of it, am severe. It asks for more. The clitoris sticks its nose out, bare, like a tongue of fire. I succumb. I want it. I want myself. I induce a sublime erection with my thumb. My clitoris lodges against the charitable and understanding index finger bracing its hardness. Its intoxication. I tightly squeeze the mound of water and fire as if to punish it. My genitals have conquered me. They are happy, and I'm shaking from head to toe with rapture. What moves me more than anything else is its tender white surface. I am orgasmic from and because of these naked sexual organs mocking me. They are so beautiful that I understand why someone would want to stick his tongue in there. I am not masturbating—I am making love to the ingratiating animal that is shamelessly coming in my fingers. It won't stop flowing, keeps telling me, "More . . . more." I could die laughing—I have fallen in love with my own cunt. In one night, I have covered seven leagues in stride and crossed through the mirror to meet myself at last.

I saw Driss again the next day, and the next, and every day thereafter. He did whatever he wanted with my body, and,

dumbfounded, I watched the marvels he created unfolding. Every word, every look swept away another fear, another bit of ignorance, another shred of false modesty. My skin was becoming more yielding, my breath more relaxed. I couldn't get enough of learning, inhaling galaxies and spitting out black holes.

I was happy, and Aunt Selma knew it. She didn't approve of my choice but blessed my body exhaling its rare essences in perfect harmony with the climbing plants in her courtyard. One day, while we were hosing down her bedroom, she suddenly stopped wiping the tiles, rearranged her scarf, then said pensively:

"Make sure you don't get pregnant. Not so much for yourself as for the kid. Infidels are cruel to bastard children."

I didn't know how to avoid a pregnancy. She must have guessed that because she returned to the attack later in the day while rolling dough into thin ropes, a flour sifter between her legs.

"The choice is yours—you can either try the Arabic recipes or ask that doctor of yours how the Europeans do it."

I knew she was worried and took her hand to kiss it. She pulled it back brusquely, smiled, conquered:

"I am really furious. Crazy mad!"

"Aunt Selma, love is a beautiful sin."

"When it comes from both sides."

"It's beyond any reason!"

"But Driss is perfectly reasonable. A solid bourgeois such as he will never marry a farm girl! Do you really think Tangiers would let you get away with that? He is a doctor, he is rich, famous, and generous with women. Mothers are ready to lick his ass so he will marry their daughters. They're even prepared to land in his bed to make him their son-in-law!"

"What do you mean? That would be *h'ram,* seven times forbidden by God, not just once!"

"God can forbid whatever He wants, but His creature still does what comes into his head. Just try and ask Him to remove the beast disguised as a man or woman from your path! And, above all, please remember that He forgives a great deal, but He doesn't particularly care for being offended. A child that has no name is an abhorrent thing! Don't make a child the world doesn't want, even if you want it. Don't kill me before my time, Badra, I still have many things to do!"

I looked at my belly and smiled; I didn't feel endowed with any talent for motherhood. All I wanted to do was love and fuck Driss. I didn't dare say that to Aunt Selma, and that's a pity.

Just as, many years later, I didn't tell her that if I was never able to bring a child into the world, it was for want of having found the father to shield it.

Driss had changed my language and my appearance, my way of thinking. I was not committing any sin, I was not stealing anything from anyone—besides, I was convinced

that the world wasn't worth a penny without the enormous inferno of love in which I stood, my heart bared. My heart loved Driss and would think about the beggars who stretch their hand toward God and are rebuffed by distracted and stingy people. I gave bread every Friday to the old people covered with blisters and dressed in rags at the entrance to the mausoleums. My conscience was clear, just as when I was at school and used to give a coin to Hay, the beggar stationed in front of the mosque in Imchouk. My heart loved Driss and shouted at the top of its voice: "Out, out, Imchouk! Out with the bigots who prefer marabouts to prophets, trances to prayers, and incantations to Koranic verses. Out with fragmented and malicious minds, the cloven-hoofed and the imams! Welcome to God, to wheat and to olive trees! Welcome to hearts pierced by love and behinds blessed by the holy water of the stars."

Driss and I would meet in his apartment on the boulevard de la Liberté, one of the many pieces of real estate he owned in Tangiers. My man managed an immense fortune, bequeathed to him by his grandmother, who was originally from Fez and whose only grandson he was. In spite of the daughter she had, she insisted on designating him as her heir and raising him to a rank that, according to the legal regulations, the premature death of her father should have prevented. Impassioned and boisterous, he explained the subtleties of Muslim law to me and how his grandmother had been able to circumvent its mechanisms, thanks to a fatwa by a mufti in her district. But money only made him laugh. Though he did not have to work, he loved his profession as a cardiologist, which he practiced with a staggering talent that was recognized equally by his peers and by his patients.

"I accepted Grandmother's money only because I knew that she and I could never be lovers. She wanted me to be brilliant and sent me to an Arab secondary school when it

was fashionable to keep the seats of French school desks warm. She was a damned fine woman!"

Driss loved Morocco to the point that he refused to open a private practice in the city, feeling that his real place was in the public health system. It was for that reason only that he had left Fez and settled in Tangiers. Sometimes he would put on the singer Oum Koulthoum and declare that he was passionate about Arabic literature and madly in love with the libertines of the classical age. I read Abou Nawas under his hungry and limpid gaze, discovering a freedom there that is not of this world. It was my lover who first spoke to me of the Passion of Hallaj. Thank God, I didn't care. Just as I didn't care about the illustrious people he listed for me, Europeans "madly in love with Tangiers, the lazy slut, and her wide-open legs, half Turkish delight, half dirty pig, reputed to cure them from death"—among whom there was a certain Paul Bowles, who lived not far away, a certain Tennessee Williams in the Minzah district, and a certain Brian Jones, who had moved in with the musicians of the musical group Jajouka.

Sometimes I would lose myself in the task of describing Driss. He wasn't really handsome. But he was provocatively lean, with long, fine muscles that played beneath his terra-cotta–colored skin and made me melt, my legs trembling and my panties immediately wet. The slender and delicate shape of his fingers made you guess he had a deadly sex organ, the kind that rides the high seas, insatiable and tireless. I am one of those for whom once is not enough, and it was he who made me discover that.

He would laugh, and his teeth made you want to bite into his full lips, inhale the space that separates the nose from the mouth, where tobacco leaves subtle traces, where I want to use my tongue. Ever since that time, I have loved the smell of tobacco when mixed with the light sweat of dark skins.

My man spent most of his free time reading and polishing jokes for his high-society evenings. He talked about women, their asses and breasts, without blinking, was funny and fierce, his penis upright and his hand fondling. He would drink, sway, scratch his butt, wander around his apartment naked and completely at ease, laugh when I'd ask him to look away and not stare at my behind when I went off to the bathroom. He paid no attention to either time or money. As for me, I was pacing the fields of childhood, overwhelmed. I wasn't in Tangiers. I wasn't anywhere. I was inside an incredible and total love, a global love that needed neither a child nor marriage, a love that knew nothing but how to love.

One day he took my face in his hands and, slightly troubled, asked me:

"Tell me, do you love me?"

I didn't know what to answer. It was of no consequence that I said this to myself or confided it to Aunt Selma. But admit it to Driss!

"I don't know!"

"Then why do you come to see me at the risk of having all of Tangiers treat you like a whore?"

"Tangiers doesn't even know me!"

125

"Oh, yes, it does, kitten! And the city knows me way too well to forgive me!"

"Forgive you for what?"

"For preferring you over Aïcha, Farida, Shama, Naïla, and any number of other wild girls of good families!"

"But you still see them!"

"That's all for a laugh, my little apricot! For a laugh! Shama claims she smells you in my hair, and Naïla says that I've been reeking of fenugreek these past few months!"

"And you believe them?"

"I have no trouble believing it where my hair is concerned! I've got my head stuffed between your legs all the time! They know that, anyway."

"No!"

"Yes! I've even suggested to them they do the same instead of spending their life taking turns sucking off Jalloun, the neighbor!"

"You are completely mad!"

"Not at all! I'm only telling you what goes on between the walls of the fine mansions in our dear city. In the meantime, would you please let your lover taste you again?"

It served no purpose whatsoever to protest or claim not to like it. All he had to do was slip my panties halfway down to find an impudent fountain.

Badra at the School of Men

When I was ten, I stopped wanting to discover women's private parts. I wanted to see a man's cock. A real one. I told my cousin Noura, and she burst out laughing, treating me like a dimwit.

"I've already seen quite a few of them and in every color!"
"Where?"
"But in the marketplace, of course! The farmers sit straddled and let their dongs hang down between the bunches of vegetables."

We went there together, made the rounds of stands without success. I was afraid we'd go home empty-handed, but then we came across a farmer who had his old djellaba pulled up high. Some blackish thing seemed to be dangling between his legs, but we weren't really able to check it out, for the old man guessed what we were up to and ran after us saying we were "the bad seed."

Moha, the potter, must have been following the episode from afar because he smiled broadly as we passed by and made a cautious sign.

"Hey, girls! Take a look here at the piece of licorice I have."

A purplish round tip emerged gingerly from the opening in his wide pants, half hidden by the tall tower of clay he was moving with regular kicks. We stopped, Noura and I, terrified for a moment, and then we bolted, shaking with nervous laughter.

As we cut across the fields to go home, I told Noura that the potter's thing was not exactly pretty to look at.

"And you haven't even seen the whole thing! Sometimes he hides in the thicket near the wadi and shows it to the little girls lingering there after their mothers have finished doing the laundry."

"Would you want to touch something that black?"

"In all honesty, yes! It seems that when you press on it, milk comes out. If a woman drinks a mouthful of it, she gets pregnant."

"No way! That happens through the eyes."

"What do you mean?"

"Well, Aunt Selma often says to Uncle Slimane, 'Stop looking at me like that or else you'll make me pregnant'!"

"Shit! Bornia is a real liar! She never stops telling my mother to stuff my father with eggs fried with garlic and raw honey so

that his thing will fill up with milk and she can have two hand-some twin boys, black as prunes and huge like my grandfather!"

Noura supplied me with juicy stories. Like the one about Sidi Driss, who had a mania that made him rub his dick against a hedge of prickly pears, since his hairy monster organ was insensitive to thorns. But not to donkey bites apparently, because he had to be taken to the emergency room the day a wandering donkey confused his glans with a fig and bit into it with bestial greed.

Noura suggested we inspect the peckers of our cousins. I shrugged disdainfully. I already knew what my brother Ali's looked like. I'd been introduced to it on several occasions when he was running after the chickens in his bare ass. I even watched him being circumcised and join the tribe of Abraham, covered with mucus and presents. The only interesting thing in the whole business was seeing my mother enthroned in the courtyard, one foot in water and the other on the ground. When Ali screamed, she moved her right foot, hitting the sides of the bucket with her ankle bracelets. The sounds of the metal and the ululations covered Ali's crying, but she was dripping with sweat, haggard, and wan. Mothers don't tolerate it when their sons, their war booty, are being touched. When all is said and done, all they really like is peckers. They go wild over them and spend their life pampering them only to use them, at the

129

opportune moment, as just so many daggers and foils. Who-ever said that women were deprived of a cock?

Noura and I were able to satisfy our curiosity about peckers when Aunt Touriyya, who lived in a neighboring village, came to visit us during the Eid, accompanied by her two boys of twelve and thirteen. At siesta time, Noura and I went to the bedroom, all mine since Naïma's recent marriage, and closed the door.

We were playing in a corner when the two cousins came in stealthily, telling us to stay calm. They quickly had us pinned against the wall, pinching our breasts and behinds. Noura was choking and tried to push Hassan away. Saïd was pulling my skirt up. He tried to mollify me:

"You want me to show you my bird?"

Noura, almost in tears, threatened she'd scream. The two brothers let go of us, and Hassan contemptuously said:

"Hey, you little pissers, we don't force anyone! But if you want to learn how to live, come and join us tomorrow near the well of Karma. Then you'll really see something!"

Against all better wisdom, we went. Saïd and Hassan were waiting for us at the edge of the village in the shade of an olive tree. First we were in a clearing, then in front of a hedge of reeds.

"Sshhh! Lower your head so they won't see us!"

What I saw through the reeds took my breath away—a dozen boys, cousins and playmates, were lying down on the

grass, the hand of one coming and going between the legs of the next one, eyes closed and breathing hard. Noura was staring with wide-open eyes. I knew I was out of place and shouldn't be watching a spectacle like this.

"Nosy one! Little pervert!" Saïd whispered, eyes bright.

"Why are they doing this?" Noura asked, obviously out of her depth.

"Because they have a hard-on, and goats aren't always docile," Hassan answered with a chuckle.

We quickly left in spite of the boys' protestations.

"Hey, girls! Now that you've been entertained, you have to reward us! Show us your pussy! Just a little of it! Come on now, don't be mean!"

I took to my heels with Noura right behind me. Furious, the boys pursued us through the thickets and would have caught up with us if Aziz the shepherd had not passed, straddling his donkey and singing Berber melodies in his deep voice. Disgusted, Saïd and Hassan had to beat a retreat.

"You two dogs, you've got it coming! We're going to tell everything to Am Habib, the tahhar. *He'll come and shorten it a second time!"*

Seeing boys touching each other shocked me deeply. So a little pecker had no special preference—it went indifferently after pussies and boys' flies. I felt brutally dethroned and horribly useless.

I said this to Noura, who sheepishly confessed:

"I actually thought that only girls did this among themselves!"

"What?"

"Well, yeah. . . . We've not asked you to participate in our games because we were afraid your mother would catch us! She's really terrifying, your mother, you know!"

"You're a real traitor! You'll pay for that!"

"I promise I was just waiting for the right moment to show you!"

"Fine, you'll have to show me very soon! Come to the house, and I'll make sure to put a stop to Mother's watchfulness."

And so they came, four girl cousins and schoolmates. We got together with our dolls and trinkets, playing grown-up ladies receiving visitors and partying. Each of the little girls, with a napkin on her head like a haïk, *knocked on my bedroom door and came in, uttering the usual polite phrases:*

"How are you, ya Lalla? *How is the master of the house? And your oldest daughter, is she married yet? May God bless your home!"*

I got them seated on a mat, at the foot of the bed. I served some leftover tea mixed with water and dry cookies I'd stolen from Mother's cabinet, and then Noura announced that we would continue our conversation under the bed. She was the first to start, pressing herself against Fatima, and then the other two

girls followed their example. I simply watched. It didn't take Noura long to abandon her playmate and deal with me. I closed my thighs, but her hand quickly found my private parts and began to titillate my bud under my dress. As if to take revenge for the delicious sensations her caresses were providing me, I shoved my hand between her legs and did the same to her. There wasn't a sound to be heard, but hands were playing a delirious score on consenting bodies. A sweet and dizzying warmth flowed down my legs. My pussy was rising beneath the active hand rubbing it, kneading the little snail hidden away at the top. I tried not to slow down the movement of my finger so that Noura would go on rolling her eyes, wild, mouth open, her forehead covered in sweat. I thought again of the scene with the boys and wondered if they had the same thrill playing their game as we did. Noura's hand was caressing me, and it was divine.

For almost a year, a kind of frenzy overtook us, urging Noura and me to rub against each other at the least opportunity, alone or in the presence of the other little girls. Her finger became the visitor attracted by my intimate spot. Already faithful, already exclusive, I was repelled by hands other than hers. Without ever undressing, our private parts barely showing, we managed to ride each other, pubis locked together and hands prying. Noura became my gentle secret. I was her idol and somewhat her property.

Saïd continued to hang around me. A few days before leaving to go back to his village, he found me, his eyes shining, and said in a begging voice:

"I have to ask you something."

"I'm listening!"

"You know what I helped you discover."

"Are you talking about those boys? So what? You're nothing but a bunch of degenerates, and women don't want anything to do with that!"

"Degenerate or not, they certainly baffled you. But that's not what I wanted to talk about. I want you to do me a favor. Come with me."

He headed toward the fields.

"Where are you going? Mother doesn't like it when I hang around with boys."

"It won't take long."

A few minutes later, we came out in the same clearing as the time before. A group of boys had gathered as if it were market day.

"You really are tiresome. You're not planning to replay the same scene?"

"No. I've made a bet."

"What bet?"

"Showing them your pussy."

I almost choked.

"I beg you! Don't let me down! You risk nothing, I assure you. You're going to stay here, nice and quiet. I'm going to use this towel as a curtain. My friends are going to stand in line. Every time I raise the curtain, you'll raise your skirt and show your pussy."

I wanted to know what would happen and let him do with me as he wished. He attached the towel to a branch, spread it out so that it covered me completely, and yelled to his buddies:

"Get ready. When I give the signal, Farouk, you take one step forward!"

And that is how I was able to exhibit my jewel for a good half hour and see the effect it had on the boys, my panties in one hand, my other hand busily raising and lowering my skirt. My cousin lifted the curtain, then let it down like a torero waving his cloth before the stunned beast. I serenely watched the inquisitive kids. They were seeing nothing but my vagina, and they were hypnotized. Some of them were blushing up to their ears; others turned pale as if they were about to faint.

When the last spectator was gone, Saïd patted me proudly on my cheek and cried out:

"Ah, cousin! You were fantastic. I have to say, you really have nerve! I'll make it up to you, I promise, I swear!"

"You bet that I'd show my pussy to your friends without lowering my eyes, is that it?"

"Better than that! Each one of these idiots paid me a coin to be able to admire your pussy. All in all, I have a whole dirham in my pocket, and to make them angry I'm going to buy the ball that Lakhdar, the grocer, has hanging on the door of his store."

My pussy for a ball! I thought the whole business ridiculous but was flattered that it had been so profitable without my having to make any effort. Still, I asked:

"And what do I get out of it?"

"The respect of your cousin, who will perhaps marry you one day."

"I don't want to marry you. You are too fat, and you smell of garlic like your mother."

We did not marry each other. He married Noura and forgot to get hard on his wedding night. More important, he would become one of the best merchants of his generation.

From the beginning of our relationship, Driss insisted on giving me a hundred dirham at the end of each month, my "salary," he said. He wanted to endow me with financial autonomy to allow me to stabilize my relationship with Aunt Selma and confirm my own position as "major and adult." The idea seemed incongruous to me, but I did not refuse his money. He was anxious for me to register for a course in stenography, to pick up my studies again, to go back to working on French and reading. I did, not overly convinced by his arguments but eager to please him.

I stopped wearing the veil and exchanged it for the dresses he gave me, the pumps, shawls, and jewelry that cost a fortune. Aunt Selma grumbled, "Since he's fucking you and keeping you, what's preventing him from asking you to marry him? He's busy making a high-class whore of you."

Marriage? But we were husband and wife, and it wasn't the piece of paper to be signed before an *adoul* that would change anything much, my lover asserted. I believed him. Before

making love, he made me read whole pages of Lamartine, corrected my diction and spelling mistakes.

"If you apply yourself, you'll soon be up to Racine!" he said, beaming.

"For what purpose? What good will all this confusion do me?"

"It will help you go deep inside your head. Earn a living, too."

"Me work? But I don't have any diplomas."

"You already have your school certificate and a few years of middle school. Let me deal with it. Soon you'll be sitting behind a desk and signing all sorts of useless documents."

He kept his word. Less than a year later, he found me a job as a secretary in one of the kingdom's airline agencies. My remuneration was ludicrous, but I was more than a little proud of bringing home a salary. Aunt Selma refused to let me give her the whole sum at the end of the month:

"It's your money, and you should feel free to do with it what you want. You want to share the expenses? Fine, but learn how to manage your finances and to save so you'll never have to face any need."

Driss also opened a savings account for me at the post office. Later, I had a bank account, but even today I keep my postal booklet like the background radiation of a long-vanished planet.

I loved Driss and learned to say so to him, ingenuous and sated with his body. He would smile, a little sad, and pat my cheek in fatherly fashion:

"My little girl, to love, what is that? Our skins are happy rubbing against each other. Tomorrow you'll meet another man, you'll want to caress his neck, have him between your legs. I'll be written off."

Aghast, I cried out, "Never!"

"Don't say silly things! I, too, could meet a woman, women, want to lick them."

"I don't like it when you're being crude."

His language reminded me of my shrewish sisters-in-law and, I don't know why, the sad fate of Imchouk's prostitutes, the *hajjalat*.

My Beloved Cast-Offs

My cousin Saïd had made me see that sex could be sold and produce money—the hajjalat *had done that and had been banished from the village. Aunt Taos accused them of "turning their pussy into cash." I was intrigued and said to myself, "So they do what I did, and I am just like them. Why all the fuss about so little?"*

The women whose names people only whispered in indignation while muttering their aoudhu-billah, *were women who had no men and by that mere fact were considered to have no virtue. There were just three of them, a mother and her two daughters, but their sins—so people mumbled—were as immense as the earth. They had been living alone ever since the father, having left on a pilgrimage, disappeared. Some said he had died in the Holy Land, while others hissed that he had settled down in Casablanca and that his females were "working" for him. How could women be "working" while they were hermits? Well, now I knew.*

I kept my ears peeled to glean every little rumor circulating about these women, feverishly and eagerly collecting them. I invented any old pretext to prowl around their house, a farm with a red-tiled roof that had been given to them by a former colonial, with a view over the wadi. They had built a white wall around the place with wild grass growing up and over it, which concealed the facade and with its snarled branches formed a screen for the ladies.

On the corner stood a dark man with a huge head who acted as their guard. He also served as their messenger. He would vanish when night fell to leave room for the guys from the village who came one by one, more or less discreetly.

Sometimes we would see the two sisters in the streets of Imchouk. Never the mother. Fully veiled, showing only one eye heavily blackened with kohl, they'd cross the square. The gossip went that they were hideously ugly, with a flat pelvis, an ashen complexion, a heavy gait, and flat feet.

It would occasionally happen that one of them visited Arem the seamstress, or entered the mausoleum of Sidi Brahmin alone. They also used to go to the hammam, and everyone knew that when the hajjalat *approached, the other women would leave the great hall to find refuge in the vestibule.*

I was able to get my fill of marveling at them the day I passed them in front of the hot water basin. As soon as she

saw them, my mother quickly turned around and almost fled. But I stayed put to devour them with my eyes. They were beautiful twins. Their bodies in tightly fitting slips of fine lace were as white as alabaster. Their outrageously heavy breasts had pink nipples that bloomed like pomegranate seeds. The color of their eyes was indefinable under the crescent-moon arch of their eyebrows. Were these the monsters people couldn't stop insulting and cursing in every corner of Imchouk? In my adolescent eyes, that flesh, those rumps, skins, and bellies were nothing other than the incarnation of complete and tyrannical desire. As I bent over to pick up the bucket filled with boiling hot water, I brushed against the leg of one of the sisters. When I raised my head, my face burning and my vision blurred, I saw her smile, a distant queen. She took my face in her hands like a cup and kissed me almost on the mouth, very lightly at first, then with warm and insistent pressure. Her lips made me dizzy. I fled, crying out. The Queen of Sheba was laughing behind my back, the same queen for whom my teacher had such special affection.

"Come back whenever you want, little girl! Your saliva is like sugar and honey," she said to me, unafraid of the world and its gallows.

My mother was waiting for me in the hall, frowning and looking suspicious:

"*What were you doing inside? Why did you take so long to come out? Didn't I tell you not to look at those disreputable girls?*"

"*I slipped as I was trying to get away! I think I may have fainted.*"

That was only half a lie, as my head was still buzzing with the pleasure I had tasted under Imchouk's very nose. The girl's kiss was burning at the corners of my mouth and made my head spin. That night in bed I couldn't help beseeching God:

"*Help me become a* hajjala! *Make that girl come to me and kiss me again!*"

She never came back except in my dreams when I was thinking about my oath to have the most beautiful vagina in Imchouk and on the entire earth. From that moment on, I knew that the hajjalat *surpassed me in beauty and mystery, but I didn't hold it against them. On the contrary. Bewildered, I sensed that they were my sisters, older sisters who would be able one day to open wide the doors of a paradise that was unimaginable to other mortals.*

One afternoon I passed one of the sisters when I came out of school. She was crossing the wadi. I decided to follow her, even if it meant my mother would disembowel me. She was walking unhurriedly and didn't turn around, looking straight ahead, her veil rustling. When she passed the mosque, she suddenly picked up speed so that I had to run.

*She went toward the cemetery, glanced around, then en-
tered it. I crouched down behind a small copse with two graz-
ing goats. Bowing down over a tomb, her palms open and
raised to heaven, the* hajjala *was praying. There wasn't a soul
around.*

*She went on endlessly reciting her verses, and I was begin-
ning to get curvature of the spine. My lateness would result in
a nice thrashing, I thought nervously. Suddenly, from the other
side of the cemetery, I saw a man emerge and go toward the
young woman. Once he was close to her, he stretched out his
hands as if to pray but then unexpectedly pulled her to him and
tilted her down onto the tomb. He slipped behind her and flat-
tened himself against her back. Hiding both bodies from view,
the veil just barely suggested the man's back-and-forth motion.
The meaning of their movements finally dawned on me, and
I left the shrubbery, turning back and thinking of a reasonable excuse for my lateness.*

*My mother didn't believe a word of what I told her. She
locked me in the toilet after giving me the worst beating of my
life. Only Aunt Selma's unexpected visit spared me from more
severe punishment. Slimane's wife made me promise never to
dawdle again after school. The next day she took advantage of
our being alone in the back of the house, surrounded by jars of
olive oil, couscous, and dry meat, and asked:*

"*Is it true that you went all the way to the cemetery last night?*"

"*Who told you that?*"

"*Squinty Tidjani told your uncle, who let me know this morning when he came home with the fritters for breakfast. What were you doing there at dusk?*"

"*I was following the* hajjala," *I confessed, blushing.*

"*What? Where do you know that woman from?*"

"*I saw her with her twin at the hammam.*"

Aunt Selma was flushed with anger. Without any further ado, she pulled my ear.

"*Listen to me: Never get near those women again. Don't you understand they're bad?*"

"*They are so beautiful, Aunt Selma!*"

"*And what's that to you? You're not going to marry one of them, as far as I know! I mean, really! I'll chop your head off if I ever catch you around them again!*"

I brought a portion of couscous to the kitchen. Behind my back Aunt Selma was mumbling, "Beautiful, she says! We know that all too well! We're going to have to marry that little girl off as soon as possible! She's capable of paying money like a man just to feast her eyes on the titties of those hajjalat!"

Suddenly quite interested, I pricked up my ears—what if I collected enough money to have those beauties show me their

breasts at their leisure—and, who knows, maybe even their adult cunts? After all, Saïd had accumulated a whole dirham in less than half an hour, thanks to my pussy. I could do the same and even better.

Noura burst out in tears when I talked to her about this:

"They'll kill you if you do that. And then I'll be all alone, a real hajjala *without you!"*

"You know, you're beginning to get on my nerves. Not everyone's a whore who wants it! I just want to know if my genitals are as beautiful as theirs!"

"But who told you they have beautiful pussies?"

"When you have a face that luminous, obviously your cunt is, too!"

"Well, in that case, you have the most beautiful pussy in Imchouk! You even have a beauty mark down there! Just like the one on your chin."

"What do you know about pussies! You specialize in peckers! And now, wipe your nose if you don't want me to go see those whores right away!"

Later I heard Aunt Taos thundering at Uncle Slimane, whose two wives had grounded him, "Your hajjalat *will come to a bad end! Just remember I told you so." Three months after my wedding, the news hit the village like a lightning flash: Aziz the shepherd had found one of the sisters in an abandoned*

field near the cemetery. Her private parts had been burned and her throat cut. Nobody ever found out who had committed the despicable act. "Undoubtedly one of her clients who couldn't make her give up her profession," my mother said calmly when I brought her the news.

I felt sad and completely nauseated. What is holy providence good for if it allows the death of a hajjala *and lets someone like Hmed destroy flower buds with complete impunity? I was shaking with suppressed rage and biting my fists in helplessness.*

The two other hajjalat *were never seen again. People say they left Imchouk one night when it was pouring rain, going in the direction of the nearby desert. I never knew which one of the sisters died, whether it was the one who kissed me in the hammam or the one who watched her do it. The fact remains that I never cut a rose again. I'd rather watch it open, bloom, wither, and die on the branch.*

Today, as I make my nightly rounds near the Harrath Wadi, I sometimes hear the stones lament. Drops of water spurt from them like tears shed too late over greatly cherished people. I then forget Driss, whom grace deserted, and see my hajjala *again in a halo of gold and mystery.*

Driss intrigued me and gave me cold sweats, unique and manifold, constant to the point of obstinacy, and as changeable as quicksilver. He was often amorous, gallant, lyrical, and generous with his time and money. And most of the time solitary, curt, egotistic, hurtful, and cynical. Capable of crying on my shoulder as he made love to me, he was perfectly crass as soon as I risked baring my heart, kissing the palm of his hand. He actually made fun of my feet occasionally, saying they were peasant feet, at the very moment he was taking off my slippers to have me try on the high heels he had just brought back from the finest shoemaker in town. One day he'd find me too fat for his taste, the next day too skinny. Sometimes he'd go on strike, refusing to touch me for three weeks straight, treating me like a lascivious female and vomiting his whiskey all over the tile floor as soon as I made so bold as to take his hand and put it on my bosom. Then, all of a sudden, as I was growing desperate at the thought of never again seeing his chest and behind, he would whisk me off my feet like a tornado, press me down on the floor, back against the wall, across an

old desk, shrieking his joy and asking me to whisper dirty things in his ear. He imposed his whims on me, once had me chase across town dying of anxiety after a phone call saying he was tired, disgusted, and on the verge of suicide. I already imagined him dead, bloodless, rigid, and there he was, receiving me with a smile, freshly shaven, perfumed, his fly open and his penis ready for battle. He inhaled my tongue, bit my breasts and lips, spread my legs, stuck his cock inside my ecstatic pussy, moving it in and out methodically, taking his time, mopping my passion with a flap of his shirt that smelled of lavender and had his initials delicately embroidered on the front pocket.

He began to talk to me about men. Then about women. Innocent as a child reciting his first lesson, he suggested a session with three, then five people. I told him he was insane and wanted to leave immediately.

He laughed, found me naive, challenged me to prove I had a soul and that there would be resurrection after death. I was appalled. To me, it went without saying we had a soul. It was obvious. And even if I didn't know exactly what God looked like, I was convinced He was omnipotent, omnipresent, and that He stabilized the planets. I had blind faith. He tried to laugh, too, cramped in his life and innately sad.

One day, with me on his lap, he whispered:

"All right, so you have a soul, but why insist on a heart? Do you know what that is, a heart?"

"A pump!"

"Ah, my little Bedouin is improving! Yes, that's it exactly! A pump. You admit I do know something about that."

"I recognize you are a fine doctor!"

"Keep quiet, traitor! I am in the best position to know that when the pump stops working, people stop existing and bodies hurtle straight into decay."

"Aunt Selma's geraniums don't ask themselves questions like that."

He opened his eyes wide, visibly startled.

"What do geraniums have to do with all this?"

"I love their color and despise their smell, but they exist without my having to make any decisions about them. Surely they, too, must have a soul even if I don't see it."

"You mean they have a meaning. And what about my penis? Does it have a meaning in your eyes?"

"Driss, you scare me. Sometimes I tell myself you and God are the same. Too much power! Too seductive! I love you so much that making love seems to me to be the only prayer capable of rising to heaven and being written down in the register of all my actions that are worthy and justified in the eyes of the Eternal."

He burst out laughing.

"You're bordering on polytheism, little one! Be careful not to burn your wings! Ah, my little heathen, my darling little pagan, my treasure, my immaculate little whore, my fearless child!"

I knew I was living in pagan territory, that my faith had disappeared between my legs, daunted by the fact that bodies can give each other such pleasure. I knew I had crossed a divine line after crossing a social line, one that had cost me nothing. I knew that in Driss's hands I regressed into a creature from before the time of Jesus, before the Koran, before the Flood. That from here on in, I was addressing myself directly to God, without any books or messiahs, without halal or *haram*, without a shroud or a burial place. I had guessed as much the evening that, as I was leaving the office, I prayed to God to let Driss make love to me again that very night after two months of nothing. God granted my wish, because at four o'clock Driss phoned me, all sugar and honey, saying he missed me wildly and that he'd take me out to dinner to one of the finest restaurants in the city.

Throughout my childhood, I was made to do nothing but celebrate saints, attend the Eid feasts, and watch the blood of rams flow across the floor for the glory of some unknown person named *Moulay* This or That. With Driss I discovered that my soul lay sheltered between my legs and that my vagina was the temple of the sublime. He claimed to be an atheist. I claimed I was a believer. Such crap! Out of love for Driss, I accepted playing chess with God. He made the opening moves. Masterful. I would build my defenses around a madman, a castle, and the queen that I was not. It is strange—I never paid any attention to the king. I

believe that God loves His lovers who, even in death, continue to bow down before His glory. I believe that God loves us to the point of watching over our sleep even when we snore.

My man wanted us to go out, to the theater, the movies, the country club. He wanted us to be invited as a couple by his friends, as well as by those outlandish circles he told me about, where everything could be said and anything could happen, so he told me. I agreed to go with him, bad tempered and totally impervious to the crowd and the liquor. That is where he began to lose me. That is where I lost him.

Driss knew I was in love and was playing with my passion. On those evenings, he loved sniffing one girl's neck, clasping another one's hips, kissing someone's temple or conspicuously pinching a pair of big buttocks. He never touched me in public and pretended not to notice my fury or the bullets I imagined shooting at the skin of his little chicks. The burning flashes going through my belly every time he was within a yard of me filled me with tears and exasperation.

One night he took me to the house of two women whose name he told me on the third-floor landing of a posh apartment building on the avenue de l'Istiqlal. He asked for French wine, took a bunch of grapes from the fruit bowl, told two or

three jokes, and then said he wasn't getting enough love. Five minutes later, Najat, who was nearsighted but had the body of a goddess, was on his lap and he was brazenly pawing her breasts. I was ready to kill when I heard Saloua, her companion, laugh and encourage him:

"'Take out her left tit. Go ahead, bite her nipple. Not too hard, though. Lick it, old friend, lick it! Najat loves being sucked. Don't you worry, she's already sopping wet. Just put your finger in there to see if I'm lying. Oh, Driss, be careful with my woman! She is too far open, too wide! But she smells good! I can smell your breath, my lovely, my adulterous vulva! Open up so that Driss can finally see that enormous cunt that tyrannizes my nights and fills my days with a woman's come. Hey, Driss, Najat only likes men when I watch her do it. She tells me that every time she has a man give it to her while I watch, my clitoris grows another centimeter. She is absolutely convinced that as long as she inhales my pussy between her lips every night, I'll end up with a cock between my legs, just to fuck her deep inside, she says, and rid her of men forever. Well, now, Driss, are you going to get on with it, or should I take your place? I want my woman, you dirty doctor who gets it up for a couple of lesbians!"

I stood up, almost stately, almost in control of myself. There was nothing for me here in this apartment with this dissolute trio. What I saw here was not my kind of world, not my man, and not my heart. So I left. All around me Tangiers smacked of heresy. I wanted to commit murder.

Driss didn't see me for another two weeks. When he did, he didn't try to apologize but sat down facing me and, pointing to the rug littered with curios and rare books, said:

"I inherited this from my fabulously wealthy grandmother, who was as unjust as the golden wheat she'd sniff as she leaned on her cane with its silver knob, right in the middle of her ripened, sensual fields in the month of May. She was fond of having nubile fifteen-year-old girls in her big canopy bed, their breasts as hard as rocks, their genitals coal-colored and docile. She adored me and would barely hide herself from my view as she sucked the tongues of her round-as-melons peasant girls or kneaded their breasts, heavy as corncobs. My love of women comes from her. She made her courtesans wear panties and kept them for me, locked like a secret in a finely carved box. 'Take a whiff of that, you dirty little hellion,' she'd say, and with the tip of her ebony cane she'd hand me a slightly stained pair of panties. I religiously sniffed at the relic, a mad and impatient young pup. 'Now go and wash up and don't let any men put a hand on your behind. They don't know how to live, those peasants. They are merciless with roses and rosebuds and, of course, with little lambs your age.'

"One night I wanted to see what was going on. Grandmother's bedroom door was ajar and the hallway deserted. Young Mabrouka was sitting on her face, breathing heavily, her hair undone, her small rump dancing. Keeping the hymen of the little fool intact, an aristocratic and knowledgeable finger was working away on her virginal buttocks while the girl's

157

vagina was glued against the mouth of the dignified old lady with her gray, impeccable chignon. When, overcome and gratified, Mabrouka slid down against my grandmother's breasts, still firm despite her age, my grandmother turned to the door where I stood, a kid and already a man, and winked at me. She had known I was there. I withdrew, sticky and full of admiration for such boldness. The sublime old lady's power still confounds me today. She richly endowed Mabrouka, marrying her off to her tenant farmer best suited to the task. She was the first to go and retrieve the linen stained with Mabrouka's virgin blood the day after the wedding. She placed a kiss on the young bride's forehead and slipped a golden bracelet hidden in her shawl under the pillow. Once again, I was standing there, in my short corduroy pants, a ridiculous bow tie around my neck. I watched Grandmother order everyone around, second only to God, serene and fully expert in the science of the heart, the price of wheat and barley.

"'Lalla Fatma,' young Mabrouka groaned.

"'Sshh,' Grandmother cut her short. 'The pain will subside, and you will slowly come to love Touhami. You must give him lots of children, my girl. You'll be a perfect wife, you'll see.' That was the day I knew that our loves are various forms of repeated incest and that there should be no barriers between bodies. Perhaps you don't know that?"

Yes, I did know it. All the bodies I'd known before had served me for this goal: to knock down the barrier between Driss and myself. They were transitory, part of a puerile and

awkward apprenticeship. I wanted to tell him so, but I was afraid he'd think I was sullied by ugly and hasty lays, although I had never really fucked before I met him. Nor had I loved. And I didn't want to kill him.

Naïma, the Overjoyed

Because Imchouk prohibited us from having men, it inevitably pushed us into the arms of women—relatives or neighbors without distinction. It also made us into voyeurs. I saw Naïma be wed.

I had just turned twelve when the wife of the fritter salesman came knocking on our door, asking my sister's hand for her son Tayeb. He had won his stripes as a policeman, and this conferred a prestige on the family that centuries of fritter oil had not been able to ensure. The mother asked the young man to parade around the village wearing his broad kepi, moving with martial step and his chin high, his arms down by his raw-boned body. "That's the best show we've had since the Europeans cleared out of this hole!" the potter snickered. "Except to top it all off, he should have dressed his mother and sisters up as majorettes," added Kaci, the manager of the Bar of the Misunderstood.

These gibes did not reach the ears of my father, who was deeply impressed with the uniform. Since Independence, all he

asked was to swap the djellabas he tailored with a single cut of the scissors for these uniforms with their many pleats and ornate with straps, martingales, zippers, and gilded buttons. Sadly, the police force never commissioned him for their officers' uniforms, not even in papier-mâché.

My mother allowed Tayeb to come by once a week to discuss the wedding preparations with his betrothed. But she always managed to be present when the engaged couple met. On nights when she was too tired but did not dare tell the son of the fritter vendor to go away, she would put Ali in charge of the watch. Seated on the living room bench between Naïma and her cop, he proctored his sister's honor from the heights of his eleven years, proud and dedicated.

One night when I had gone to bed right after dinner, the strange deep silence that reigned over the house woke me up. My father wasn't snoring, and the wood had stopped burning. I got up and stole into the living room. The spectacle was incredible. The pair was doing battle above the head of a sleeping Ali. Then I realized that the top of Naïma's dress was unbuttoned. Her policeman was fiddling with her breasts while she was desperately trying to put them back into her bodice. I left on tiptoe, stifling nervous laughter. So there it was: All you needed was a set of breasts to make the world go crazy and forget all caution. My mother's vigilance had been royally cuckolded.

162

Voyeur, I was too perceptive when Naïma invited me to visit her in the little town of Fourga, where her husband had been stationed a few months after their marriage. Cars were seldom seen in Imchouk—you had to resort to tractors or carts to cover long distances. Tayeb's father suggested taking me to Fourga on the back of a donkey, and my mother accepted without any problem.

Chouikh felt that his one and only fortune lay in his Egyptian donkey, an animal with golden fur, highly prized all over the valley, with well-padded flanks and eyes as vicious as his master's. He propped me against his back and told me to hold on tight to his waist. He hummed all the way, ignoring me, and under the pretext of now being our father-in-law, didn't give me a single compliment. My feet dangled, happily kicking the donkey's flanks in spite of the rain that continued to fall, drenching us down to our bones.

I was happy to see Naïma again. I missed her laughter and her bride-to-be chatter.

In her tiny apartment with its black and white tiles, Naïma went barefoot. Her henna had lost its red ocher sheen and had turned as gray as Fourga's sky. But her skin seemed more luminous and her gestures slower, almost indolent. Her gait had changed, as well. She swayed her hips in a way I had never seen her do. I stared at her legs, for Noura claimed one of the

results of marriage was that the thighs of brides grow wider and consequently the legs become bowed. But Naïma didn't look as if that had happened to her.

At the end of the day, my brother-in-law came home, strapped into his uniform. The three of us had dinner together at the same table. At home, Papa always ate his meals alone. Once the chicken couscous had been downed, Tayeb yawned and went to the bedroom. Naïma told me I'd have to sleep with them because the kitchen was infested with cockroaches. She put three huge blankets on the floor and slipped one of the cushions of the couch under my head. "There, now go to sleep."

I don't know if it was my pleasure at seeing my sister again or the different bed, but I had trouble falling asleep. I was just about to doze off when their bed began to creak. Strange sounds followed the noises of the new wood.

I knew that marriage also had to do with sex, even if people were desperately trying to have us believe the contrary: If they work themselves to death to marry off boys and girls, to spend fortunes on dowries and trousseaux, to celebrate weddings at huge expense, it's only because men and women are afraid of the dark and need company. If they lock themselves in a bedroom, it's only out of habit. If they sleep in the same bed, it's

only to keep warm. If women become pregnant, it is the will of God. And if they make themselves beautiful at night, half an hour before their husband comes home from the fields or the workshop, it's only to welcome them at the door, done up with kohl and henna. Well, not exactly! Marriage, that grand affair, is also this: the creaking of box springs that comes to a crescendo, the noisy sighs of my brother-in-law, my sister's submissiveness as she opens her legs without protest. Marriage is the commands of the proprietor, short and specific: "Open wider," "Turn over," "Lie down." It is whispered words, incredible and terrifying in their truth: "It burns," "Yes, suck me," "Oh, I love you like that."

Naïma did not need to speak. Her husband was expressing his pleasure as well as hers, while the creaking mixed with their stifled hard breathing. Then came a sudden deep sigh. It was Naïma giving up the ghost. A kind of nausea together with some cramps shook my belly. My eyes filled with tears. I knew in that moment that I hated Naïma. I wanted to be in her place, under Tayeb's pubis.

The next day as I said good-bye, I avoided looking her straight in the eye. On the way back, all I did was clench my teeth and fists, saying to myself that one day I, too, would make beds creak, beds as enormous as the fields of Imchouk. I would

make my husband shout with pleasure, because my cunt would be that ardent, biting like the burning waves of the Chergui, tight as a rosebud. That is what Driss had promised me when he made his first appearance on the bridge of the Harrath Wadi.

In the half dark of Driss's apartment, siestas tasted like barley water and watermelon. My lover would read, nude, stretched out on an old Persian carpet, and I'd be daydreaming, lying diagonally with my head on his thigh. He'd burst out laughing whenever an indelicate sentence affirmed his licentious biases.

"Listen to this one: 'A cunt needs two cocks more than one cock needs two cunts.' Excellent! That is well reasoned and superbly stated. Here's another good one: 'From birth on, every cunt carries with it the names of the ones who'll fuck it.' That's perfect!"

The Umayyads of Damascus, the Abbasids of Baghdad, the poets of Seville and Cordoba, the drunks, hunchbacks, whores, acrobats, lepers, assassins, opium addicts, viziers, eunuchs, pederasts, Negresses, Seldjuks, Turkomans, Tartars, Barmecidals, Sufis, Kharijites, water vendors by auction, fire-eaters, monkey tamers, rejects, and those too stupid for words ran through bedrooms, screamed under torture, climbed the curtains, pissed in crystal glasses, and spread their come

on cushions embroidered in silver thread. I saw Driss order them to be quiet, make them go through flaming hoops, lose them in the heart of the desert, and pick them up again covered in sores and lice. I saw him eat figs split by the sun and two-toned pears, as he dreamed of orgies and dressed in brocade. He had women like Saloua and Najat under his thumb. But I had only him to adore.

They turned up one evening after he had watered me with champagne, decided to lick me from head to toe, seizing his stimulation in my navel. I could feel the orgasm rising when they rang the doorbell, slightly drunk and made-up as if they were going to a party. I barely had time to cover myself with a sheet before they settled down and lit their cigarettes. Saloua had a lecherous look, knowing I was naked and irked. Driss wasn't even trying to hide his erection.

"My word! Your woman leaves nothing for anyone else anymore! And you just can't get enough of screwing her! Wouldn't you like to give my woman a slow fuck, just for a change?"

Saloua horrified me, but, strangely, her language excited me. She talked like a man. In her corner, Najat had already unhooked her bra, and Driss was waiting for the rest, his penis jumping impatiently. A flow of lava and desire swept my belly and head.

I locked myself in the bathroom. Before getting dressed, I looked at myself in the mirror. I saw a woman disheveled and hollow-eyed. Standing up, one foot on the bathtub edge,

I took my clitoris between two fingers, hurting from the bite of desire. Swollen and in pain, it was beating like a panic-stricken heart. My fingers were sticky with a transparent liquid that smelled of cloves. In spite of my efforts, I couldn't come. I was too angry. Too much in love and too serious, as well. My head filled with dark thoughts, I tried to extricate my clitoris, my only solitary foreplay, from its niche of fur, just to see what it could do. Well, it couldn't do a thing! There it was, red and ludicrous, demanding Driss's tongue to get taut and his penis to send it into a trance.

Back in the living room, I saw the little smile of my man, the vile creature. As if he guessed what had come over me and made me leave the room with its hoarse laughter. As if he knew I had had no pleasure whatsoever in playing with myself. He kissed Najat, Saloua's official lover, full on the mouth while his hand was buried between her legs. Saloua was slumped on the couch, her back propped against the cushions. She was smoking, pretending to be distracted, almost asleep. Later on, I found out her pipe was stuffed with hashish provided by Meftah, the dwarf who was the guard of her building.

I put the record of Esmahan back on. "*Imta ha taarif imta, inni bahibek inta . . .*" The crackling distorted the voice of the Lebanese singer, Egyptian by adoption, who had died too young in a car accident. I sat down beside Saloua of my own accord to let her know she made little impression on me, and smoked my third cigarette with closed eyes. I didn't want to see Driss play with Najat's breasts or guess that his finger had

already made its way into her private spot. I jumped when I heard him say clearly, "You're not getting wet. I'm going at it with my saliva."

Saloua ostentatiously put her hand, heavy as lead, on my knee. "No," I said and got up. No, I repeated as I went up the boulevard de la Liberté to Aunt Sclma's house. No, I replied to my head that, grown dim, was defending the idea that love never sends bills and never judges. No, I shrieked in my dreams at Driss, who told me it was just a game and I was the only one he loved. When I woke up, I said to myself that Driss was a trap from which I had to escape. I knew that if I decided to dig the grave of this love, I would also have to carry its corpse, wander in the desert for forty years, and then, vanquished, recognize that, in fact, the corpse I was lugging around was my own.

Hazima, the Roommate

It was the lycée *that put Hazima in my bed, or actually, the boarding school with the rustle of the dresses of girls with their manias, their hygiene rituals, and their bickering. At home, my mother never wore skirts or bras, and I admired the effect they made. Consequently, I confused clothing and bodies, and, wanting the former, I had no scruples about admiring the latter. The young skins, cleavages, rumps that had been prominent since childhood and were now finding their place in the sun, all of it made me wildly curious and somewhat envious.*

One night, Hazima, the most beautiful girl in the boarding school and the sassiest one as well, lifted the blankets and slipped into my bed.

"Warm my back," she ordered.

I obeyed. Too mechanically for her taste because she protested:

"Gently! You're not carding wool, you know."

I caressed her skin with my moist and open palm. She really was silky. Her satin shivered, and her beauty marks crested beneath my fingers.

"Lower," she said.

I went down to the curve of her lower back. She remained taut and motionless. Then I raised myself on my elbow and leaned over to look at her. She was sleeping with tightened fists.

The next day the same thing happened, and the days following. Each time, she'd doze off or pretend to. One day, she suddenly turned over and offered me her barely budding chest. Trembling, I moved from one breast to the other. It was as if some other hand was caressing my own chest. I grew emboldened one evening and slipped a finger into her barely fuzzy vagina. She suddenly arched her back and went into convulsions, and with my other hand I had to smother her moans that sounded like a death cry. Hazima was better than Noura, more serious, more like ripe fruit.

As time went by, my nocturnal get-togethers with Hazima became routine. We claimed to be sleeping together "to stay warm," and this raised no eyebrows in the school. Once I was grown, I had to smile at the idea that, when all was said and done, the dormitory was nothing more than a purring brothel and right under the nose of the supervisors and the internal administration.

In class I was dying of boredom, since studying seemed to me a more profitable endeavor for city people than for the country girl I was. It is difficult to convert a proud descendant of illiterate generations—and proud of it—to the value of knowledge! Faced with my inertia, my teachers became incensed, but I had absolutely no urge to please them. I spent my time staring at the passing clouds and waiting for Hazima.

Still, at the end of the year, Hazima and I left each other wordlessly and without tears. At our age, loving someone did not resonate, and fiddling around with someone of the same sex didn't have any consequences. Sex was an act of indecency committed only between men and women. Hazima and I were merely preparing ourselves to receive the male.

My body, on the other hand, was changing at such a dizzying pace that it seemed impossible to catch up with. It would lie down, stretch, become wrapped and rounded even in my sleep. It resembled the country that I was told was mine, new and champing at the bit, recently separated from its colonials without being divorced from them. Textile factories were opening in the north, threatening to ruin my father, and newly sated and educated young men were beginning to find the rural areas unappreciated and too narrow for their heads stuffed with equations, socialist slogans, or pan-Arabic dreams.

After having been interested only in my genitals, I became curious about the rest of my body. I scrutinized my feet, which I thought were too flat, and consoled myself by admiring my delicate joints and my slender fingers, inherited from my mother. My chest was swelling, full of vigor and insolence. A silky down had grown over my pubic area, thick enough to peek out from under my panties at times. It now filled my hand and hit my palm like the back of a stretching cat. My skin was soft but not overly sensitive, amber colored but not brown. My eyes were almost yellow and attracted attention, as did the beauty mark on my chin. But more than my face, my body shouted its scandalous beauty.

My cunt put an end to my studies, as Hmed the notary was drooling with impatience to possess it.

He only had its rind, however, for the pulp was reserved for Driss, his teeth and his cock.

Escape. Break off with Driss. Forget desire. Admit to fear. Look it straight in the eye. Two porcelain dogs. The terror of loving. Of getting wet. Vomiting and admitting to being subject to jealousy. To hatred. Never admitting to being capable of following Driss in his escapades and whims. Not circling the pot for fear of falling into it. I was suffocating and refused to take my lover's phone calls.

He ended up by cornering me, forcing me into his black DS, and taking me to dinner by the harbor. I refused to touch the mullets and shrimp. He was getting systematically drunk on beer.

"It's either them or me!"

"It's you *and* they, at the same time, no discussion."

"I am not your object nor am I your servant. I didn't escape from Imchouk for you to treat me like dirt."

"You fled from Imchouk because it wasn't enough for you anymore. Because you missed me and you wanted me."

"It wasn't you I was looking for."

"Oh, yes it was! Me and nothing but me. With all my flaws and my cock that stands up sideways."

"I don't love you anymore."

"That's not what your pussy says when I'm in there."

"It's lying."

"A cunt can never lie."

I was glancing around, panic-stricken for fear one of the waiters would hear Driss pouring his crude vocabulary out to me. Fortunately, we were alone under the pergola, since the cool air had kept the other customers from sitting on the terrace.

"You're coming home with me tonight."

"No."

"Don't force me to yell."

"Don't force me to watch you make love to those two sluts."

"I only make love with you!"

"You're making fun of me!"

"Whoa there! You don't understand anything. You do not understand!"

"Well, what do you want? I'm just a peasant girl, and you're a far too complicated feudal lord!"

"Is that what's bothering you?"

"What bothers me is that you have absolutely no respect for me!"

He began to shout. I got up to leave. He caught me as I was going. I got into his car without a word, browbeaten. He drove at breakneck speed. At the railroad crossing, the gate was coming down and you could hear the strident whistle of a train coming from our right. He put his foot on the accel-

erator and said, "Now!" The blinding light of the train awakened me. I yelled:

"No! No, Driss! Don't ! Don't do that!"

We smashed through the gate and the car tore across the tracks ten seconds before the train passed by. A sudden turn of the steering wheel sent us into the bushes, two yards from the lagoon. The high-tension wires were glowing red and threatening above our heads. Ever since that moment, I have known what the Apocalypse looks like.

I did not cry. I did not move. Driss was breathing heavily, sniffling, his forehead against the steering wheel. After an eternity, I opened the door. I began to scratch my face from the temples down to my chin, the way I had seen the women of my tribe do when their sorrow broke the heart of heaven. Each wound raised the pitch of my lament.

"This is for your whores. For my disgrace. For my perdition. For having met you. For having loved you. For Tangiers. For fucking. For your cock. For my cunt. For the scandal. For nothing."

"Stop, I beg you! Stop that, I said! You're going to mutilate yourself!"

Blood dripped down to my elbows.

"Take me back to Aunt Selma's," I said to him, depleted.

He wiped my face and arms with one of his shirttails, drove to the nearest health center and came out with vials and compresses. I fell asleep in his arms, my cheeks daubed with iodine and healing ointment.

I didn't go outside for a week, during which time I was his child, his grandmother, and his cunt. Each time I rode him, I saw his heart, a sky in which comets flew with their snowy tails and a flaming bush in the center like a dragon. Driss was delirious under the bites of my vagina, drenched in sweat:

"Your cunt! Your cunt, Badra! Your cunt is my ruin!"

Finally, at the end of the night and of my permanent loneliness, covered with salt and sperm, I said:

"Now I will be able to watch you fuck those whores without weeping."

We went to the lesbians like two Siamese cats mewing their deceitful hunger. Najat opened the door in her robe. The air smelled of Chanel No. 5 and female orgasm. Saloua was in the living room, white and naked, her panties thrown ostentatiously over the arm of an easy chair.

She looked at me, amused, a little disdainful.

"It happens to us, too, sometimes to stay locked inside for three days in a row just to have a great time. But, you see, we aren't sectarian! We always welcome Driss with wide-open legs. Wine or champagne?"

"Water," I answered.

Najat served Driss his whiskey, put down a carafe of water, a stemmed glass, and a tray with fruit in front of me.

Saloua put her panties back on, then slipped into a silk housedress. She lit a cigarette, took a gulp from her glass of red wine, and sat down to my left between Driss and me.

"Badra, you are beautiful, but you're a dope! Dumb enough to be slapped around. You think you're the only one who loves. First of all, do you even know how to love?"

"What I know or do is none of your business."

"Obviously. But you have to admit that other people may have the same feelings as you without behaving the same way."

"I don't want to act like other people."

"Just because we do it for money, you think that Najat and I are monsters and whores. Being a whore does not mean you don't love your work. You don't love, period. I actually like men. Najat has learned to accept them. And because I love her, fucking with her is sweeter to me than getting laid by Farid el-Atrach himself."

She was beginning to exasperate me again, in spite of my fine resolutions.

"I know you're here because of Driss."

She was right on target, and she knew it from Driss's silence and my clenched jaws. Najat was doing her nails and whistling.

"I am like wine, Badra! Some day you'll come here just to figure out what it is your man gets here."

She pressed against me. "Don't touch me," I said to her. Driss stood up and looked at Tangiers through the curtains. She raised herself halfway and, traitor, held me pinned against her. With two bumps of her lower body she adjusted her genitals to meet mine and began to massage the mound in a broad and precise movement. Hazima's memory glimmered briefly beneath my closed eyelids, like a fuse. My heart was pounding wildly. I hadn't expected this. Aghast, I felt my genitals react. They were pulsating against Saloua's, crazy with desire. Not understanding what was happening to me, I felt her in-

strument dig into me. With her heavily ringed left hand, she stifled my protestations. For a full minute, I was subject to a burning rape by her finger, which she kept rigid and triumphant inside my gaping wet vagina. I was not a virgin anymore, but I was trembling with the same rage and the same shame. In a flash, I saw Driss bend over Najat. His bulging fly was eloquent enough. My second man had abandoned me. He, too, was handing me over to rape, this time by anonymous hands bereft of love.

"Let go of my lover, Driss," Saloua yelled at last, exposing the shimmering finger she had just pulled out of my body. "She's the one I want. I'm not crazy enough to think this one is getting wet over me. Come and jump her, and let's get it over with! Or else, I swear on Dada's head that I'll screw her right here under your eyes. My clit is standing up, and her pussy is suckling me beneath my panties, like the mouth of a newborn. Really, my boy, your dick shouldn't be bored frisking this one," she declared, greedy and sardonic, licking her thieving finger.

From Driss's open fly emerged a reddish ember. A drop was shimmering at its thick crest. Stupidly, I thought for the nth time that the circumciser had left him with a fine cock. In lordly fashion, he planted himself in front of me, and, ashamed and in heat, I took him between my lips. He had taught me how to suck a cock correctly. I was getting so wet that even Judgment Day was forgotten. I was getting wet and praying to the Lord, "Please, do not watch! Please, forgive me! Please,

don't forbid me to walk into Your Kingdom and pray there again! Please, deliver me from Driss! Please, tell me that You are my only God who will never abandon me! I beg You, Lord, help me leave this hell!"

To my left, Najat was shrieking as she bit the sacrilegious finger of her lover, who laughed.

"Not her! Not a woman!" Najat shouted.

A resounding blow calmed the scorned lover's hysteria. In my mouth, Driss tasted of salt, and his penis was velvety. Loving and intoxicated, I caressed his balls, which were small and hard, contracted in obvious pleasure. He didn't utter a word, happy to watch my lips slide up and my saliva flow down the length of his shaft. Contrary to my prayers, I saw God see me and condemn the stupid suffering that only humans know how to inflict on each other. I saw Him condemn those who rape children, banish Satan from His mercy, promise him He would vanquish him, humiliate him, make him parade before the entire Creation someday so that Creation would ask forgiveness that such a creature had been able to exist, then chain him up in hell without Evil being able to either laugh or weep.

Her breasts taut, her gaze distant, Najat let herself be opened by Saloua's ferocious fingers. Soon the entire hand took possession of the body yawning a moan of bitter desire and openly in love.

"You're nothing but a whore. My never-satisfied darling whore," Saloua crooned. Her nose teased the clitoris that was

standing up like a small purplish flag while her hand was working the liquefied body of her mistress, whose belly I saw furrowing in successive waves of pleasure. Driss was supporting my neck while I pumped him and wondered whether he would ejaculate in my throat when he raised my head, tender, my accomplice. He murmured, "Don't stop, please. Your tongue. . . . Your lips. . . . Tell me you're getting wet." Truthfully, I was flooded but refused to tell him that. Najat was raving, her eyes rolled upward, "Now, now! Oh, love, finish me off." With a rough push, Saloua pulled her hand away. Najat shrieked. Leaving my mouth dexterously and on his own authority, Driss placed himself in her mouth. Taken aback, I saw Saloua spread the buttocks of the man I loved and put her tongue in his anus. When the sperm burst forth in streams from the penis I loved into the mouth of my covetous rival, it was my turn to shriek, my sanity definitively shaken.

At the office, I didn't do very much, just as before at school. I was happy to put my hands on the keyboard of the old Olivetti, and, idiotic and senile before my time, I watched the building across the street. The rain was gently falling on the terraces. Drops of water rolled down, interlaced, then became strings that dripped down the shutters, making water curtains for the shops. I was dreaming of the Harrath Wadi and my family, which had become resigned to my running away when it turned out that my brother Ali's *antariyyat* had been without consequences.

What had Tangiers made me into? A whore. A whore similar in every way to its Medina, which I still liked much better than its European section, imprinted with my footsteps and those of Driss, the heedless one. The aristocrats who once lived inside the casbah had left it in favor of European-style apartment buildings and residences on the swanky hills, with their views of the sea and gloved chauffeurs to drive the sedans. They left behind sumptuous homes, with such heavy chandeliers that no modern ceiling would

be able to withstand the weight, walls painted in gold leaf, courtyards and terraces overflowing with ceramics whose patterns were fading, and paneling encrusted with stucco that only rare artisans still knew how to execute. Country people like myself, in a rush to enjoy life and rather careless about the splendor of the old days, had arrived and replaced the former owners, and the Medina was in decay, reeking of rats and adult urine.

And then I discovered the virtues of liquor. It took a while for me to settle on a choice—wine upset my stomach, beer gave me diarrhea, and champagne made me gloomy. Only whiskey with lots of water made me crackle like a birch fire and spared me any hangover. I appreciated its most unusual and most expensive labels, which made Driss laugh.

"You are right, my dove! If you're being bad just to be bad, it's always better to choose bad things that are overpriced. Never lower yourself, my almond, to revel in mediocrity and be content with the ordinary. You'd anger your guardian angels if you were to start living on the cheap."

My sins are being scooped up today, I thought. When did I last say a prayer, make my ablutions? I laughed inside my head: A pagan, I prostrated myself five times a day facing in the direction of Mecca. Converted to love and violations, I directed my supplications to God in the middle of screwing or in the shower. Me, a Muslim? What about this man, these women, the alcohol, the chains, the questions, the lack of remorse, the repentance that is nowhere to be seen? Only

the fasting of Ramadan remained intact. It purified my anguish and gave me a rest from alcohol. Naturally, Ramadan proved to be powerless in forbidding me the body of Driss, who did not observe it. Oh, he respected my penitence but didn't think it had any merit. I couldn't tell him that at sundown my first sip of water rose to Heaven accompanied by just one wish: that God accept the sacrifice of my thirst and my hunger, that He know that my body was still capable of being faithful to Him.

But I made love with Driss during Ramadan, breaking my vow and betraying my promise. All I could find to say to God was, "Don't look at me now. Look elsewhere until I am done." Done with what? This sublime and loathsome act during which Driss's penis banged my belly, oily and shimmering. We would lie in bed, my lover and I, he smoking his cigarette and I with my head on his brown chest, black with hair. I caressed him and had the impression I was running my fingers through a woman's head of hair. His sweat was the moisture of the most beautiful pussy a woman could display under the open sky. He inhaled the smoke, and I'd retrieve it, exhaled straight from his lungs, would keep it in mine and then playfully and sensually breathe it out, sodden with alcohol and nicotine. My belly was frothing and wouldn't stop dripping its excess of love and expectation into my panties and onto the sheets. I wanted to have him inside me all the time. All the time. "Stay there! Don't leave." He laughed, rooting about in my vagina, flooded with my water and his sperm. He had

transformed my lower abdomen into a mouth that wanted nothing other than to take him in and shelter him forever. Each time he began to leave, I said, "Stay," just so I wouldn't have to see my vagina spill over between my legs, ridiculous and banal. I couldn't take any more loving. I couldn't take any more wanting to leave him.

The evening before the Eid, while children ran shouting through the poorly lit alleys and set off their firecrackers against the walls swollen with humidity, Driss gave me one of his brilliant monologues, the last one before our breakup.

"You see," he said, "I love you. And I don't want that. Life is a cock. It gets up, and that's good. It becomes flaccid, and it's over. You have to move on to other things. Life is a cunt. It gets wet, and that's good. If it starts asking itself questions, you have to drop it. We shouldn't complicate existence, my nightingale. A cock. A cunt. Period. When will you finally get that?"

"I'm trying, you know. One day, if I keep listening to you, I will finally be able to leave you."

"Leave me? What for? No, you won't be able to do without this cock that gets it up for you without ever softening and never stops dripping between your buttocks without your consenting to give it your anus."

"I don't hate you enough yet to offer you my behind."

"Hate me? Really, you're awfully tiresome with those big words about love and with that tragic face of yours! You're beginning to get on my nerves with your 'I love you' and 'I

hate you,' and 'One day I'll leave you'! I have never lied to you, and I've always told you that I get hard, I take, I spurt, I come, I forget. Who is making your head swell? Who is going to your head?"

Obviously no one. Not even the recent reading that Driss had compelled me to take on, such as his Simone de Beauvoir, his Boris Vian, and his Louis Aragon. Or the pompous and pretentious French songs that he called "songs with a text." He swore only by Léo Ferré. I found the other voice, Greco's, mellower. In any case, Oum Koulthoum alone made my whole being shiver. I usually gave the rest of those voices an angry finger and an exasperated "Pfff." He treated me like an Arab stuck in a rut. Between clenched teeth I would tell him to go fuck himself.

And then Driss spoke to me about Hamid. The sky over Tangiers was blue, and it was a Sunday morning that encouraged idleness and cuddling. The copious breakfast tray reminded me that I spent more time at my lover's than at Aunt Selma's, who barely spoke to me anymore. Of course, I felt like making love, but Driss felt like doing something else. He wanted to masturbate as I watched.

The tip of his penis stood out, massive and red, and the superb shank triumphantly displayed its swollen veins, saturated with blood. I was watching, fascinated and more flustered than I wanted to admit. Driss went at it delicately, pressing the glans between two fingers, then taking hold of the entire member, his hand tender and maternal. For the first time in my life, I

became aware in the most absolutely material and physical way that my clitoris was erect and standing up ravenous between my labia. After that discovery I never again believed in female passivity. I know when I get wet, tremble, and get erect, even if my legs remain closed and my face unruffled.

Driss's hand wrapped itself around his cock, pressing it in a way I never had. He was going to ejaculate in my face without my breasts or my vagina having anything to do with it. If men can give themselves this much pleasure all alone, why do they insist on penetrating us? I wanted to cover it with my lips. He refused. "No," he said as he massaged it from the center out to the end, in love with his own cock, which he knew was beautiful.

"No, women don't know how to jerk a man off," he explained, "just to suck. And even then! It's not as good as with a man."

From then on, I also knew how to turn into a pillar of salt.

"You've fornicated with men?"

"My love, my mango and wild blueberry juice, what do you think? Yes, a man has sucked me off. And it's so good that I'm wondering if I shouldn't give up on women."

He was bulging like a donkey, protruding from his own right hand and streaming with transparent liquid.

"Why are you making that face? What about yourself?"

"What about me?"

"You didn't exactly protest when Saloua stuck her tongue down your almond the last time."

"Because monsieur preferred squirting into an almond that wasn't mine."

He laughed, kissed me full on the mouth.

"You're getting better, you know! You're beginning to talk like me. I adore your innocent young obscenity. With a bit more effort, you'll be able to stick some hemorrhoids onto the guardians of virtue. What would be ideal is if you'd write lots of exquisite vulgarities and post them on the walls. But rest assured, my virgin drenched in wetness, I am crazy about your almond, and if the urge should come over you to get it on with that old mercenary lesbian, I wouldn't hold it against you in any way."

"That's of no interest to me."

"Stop, baby, stop! I hate it when people lie to my face, and you know it. Am I lying to you when I tell you that Hamid's ass is superb? You'd think it was a pussy, it's that slippery! Not to speak of his ember!"

"I should have known you were a homo to the bone the day Saloua shoved her tongue in your behind."

"Whoa there, I'm not a fag, even if I believe that everyone should use his ass the way he wants to! And if Saloua shoved her tongue in my asshole, it's because men open up down there when they ejaculate. You have to learn it all, my dove. That bitch of a Saloua has fiddled with too many cocks and asses not to know that elementary rule of pleasure. You, on the other hand, you don't dare. You don't dare do anything."

"Have you no shame? You, you let yourself get sodomized?"

"What I like is fucking. I like pussies drooling like omelets. I like my cock there in front of you about to explode. As for your fine morals, you should know that I have never touched a child or a virgin. Where Hamid is concerned, he doesn't sodomize me. He merely gives me a taste of paradise."

"What will Tangiers say of its brilliant physician?"

He burst out laughing, opened his thighs wide, and kneaded his penis, on the point of surrender.

"You are foolish. . . . You are innocent. . . . Tangiers doesn't give a shit! All that matters is that the appearances be made! Don't make me list the married males you come across in the plushest living rooms who get themselves laid every siesta by some cute *h'bibi* in their middle-class alcove with Andalusian music or the Stones as background! May they croak with open mouths! It's a foul race that doesn't ever end coming or stop mocking. Not to mention those precious married ladies, mostly grandmothers, who love having the scarlet lips of the wellborn suck them! And then there is the lot of you down there in the sticks, in Auvergne I was going to say, you do it, too! But you don't even do it with any joy or delicacy."

So now Imchouk was in the Auvergne!

"To get back to the subject, Hamid is married and faithful to his wife. He is a professor of medieval history and knows more about Pepin the Short and Bertha with the Big Feet than anyone else. More important, he has an ass like a queen. Even his wife bites it when he takes his bath, and she rubs his back

with a very rough horsehair glove. I knew him in Fez, in a villa full of acacia trees and a splendid fountain in the middle of the patio. It was the fortieth day after the exquisite death of my cousin Abbas, and I never did stop making fun of Azraël, the angel of death, thereby shocking the sons of the deceased and disheartening his nervous friends, who were rustling their silk djellabas, shining like bidets, and bursting with false piety and the traditional formulas I despise. I refused to have any of the ritual couscous, tajines, and cakes that mark the end of the pre-scribed mourning period. The women were insipid with their permanent waves. Not one young girl around. They were locked in the kitchen and the ground-floor bedrooms, smoking their sweet tobacco and secretly caressing each other's tits. The house was huge, and my flask of whiskey was empty. I went to uri-nate, and there was Hamid. He was trembling when he caught me as I left the toilet, my cock smelling of warm piss and I al-most in a bad mood because that is how much I detest com-passion, badly tolerated grief, the whole drama and fuss of Fez. My mother pretended to be asleep, sitting upright and deceit-ful amid the *baldiyya* of her clan and her class, in the large cen-ter room done completely in yellow mosaic tile, with heavy drapes and mirrors covered in white sheets.

"He took my hand and put it on his penis.

"'One or the other. Either I ream you or you ream me,' he said.

"I burst out laughing.

"'It's the vodka,' I told him. 'I saw you upstairs, sipping away with Farid.'

"'You wouldn't want me to drop my pants in the middle of all that company, right there on the patio with all those old bourgeois who're over the hill, almost ruined, and already mummified. Touch me and you'll see if it's the vodka that gives me a hard-on.'

"I had never touched a man before. I let my hand wander across the bulge in his pants. As a challenge. For a laugh. His fly was open, and his wife was in the living room chatting with my old Aunt Zoubida. I think they were cousins a thousand times removed. We were two guys on an Arab patio, and the stars were shining brightly, near us, within hand's reach."

Driss was talking and smoking, his penis up in the air, firm and confirming. It was obvious that his hard-on was not for me.

"So?"

"What, so? You who like cocks, you would have wept at the sight of what I took out of his shorts. I pressed the shining end of it, and, suddenly sad, he whispered, 'I'm cold, and it's a beautiful night.' You ought to know that he has a strong build and is a good head taller than I.

"'A fag?' I asked, squeezing his penis.

"'Not really. A little, with the sharecroppers of the family farm and twice in Amsterdam. But what makes me hard is your face. And your mouth. You probably suck like a king, don't you?'

"'Yes, when a slit electrifies me. But you, you don't have a slit.'

"'No, but I do want to be your woman. Afterwards I'll take you.'

"'Standing or on the side?' I asked sarcastically.

"'You're putting me on,' he said, patting me on the fingers.

"In less than five minutes, a guy had picked me up, put his cock in my hands, and had an orgasm right under my nose as he told me he had wanted to get laid and would return the favor."

"So?"

Driss's penis was jumping up and down with desire, a liberated monster. He was no longer touching himself. He was looking at himself. Then he said to me:

"And what about you? You can hardly stand it, right? Obviously, no one has ever dared to tell you such horrifying things."

"So?"

"There was nothing to do in that Arab house, where the farthest nooks and crannies were lit up with imitation oil lamps. He was so sure of himself, so arrogant, that I drew him into a corner of the street and kissed him on the mouth. He got hard again up against my fly. 'You want it?' 'Yes.' 'Tomorrow, three o'clock at my apartment. Will that work for you?' 'You'll let me suck you off?' I pushed him against the wall, my cock hard: 'I will stick it up your ass right here and now if you continue to fire me up with that language of yours, spoken like a seasoned whore.' He went back to his

wife, and I went home. I didn't close an eye, flustered and not really happy that I had pushed things that far. Toward five in the morning, I decided to stand him up. At noon, my hands began to shake. At three o'clock, I opened the door before he even rang the bell.

Driss had time and money. Driss wasted them both without remorse. "Let's take a trip," he said to me. "You'll love Paris, Rome, and Vienna. Unless you'd prefer Cairo? You should go and console your Egyptian brothers for the whipping that Israel just gave them after succeeding in crossing the Barlev Line. On the head of my ancestors, and what a beating that was! No? Well then, there's still Tunis, Seville, and Cordoba. I'll take you wherever you'd like, sweetheart. I am your humble and faithful slave."

He was lying. He was playing. I didn't want to go anywhere. And, indeed, we never did travel together.

"I don't love you anymore, Driss."

"You're only now beginning to love me, my kitten. Don't be ridiculous. There are so many things we have to do together."

Other than making love, there was actually very little left for us to do together. The body is always a session behind, dreading the separations because the first one had been so painful. I hate the memory of the cells for its canine devotion that taunts the neurons and merrily scorns the cortex and its

wild fantasies. It was my head and not my body that saved me. It advised me to take an apartment right away, even if it meant that Driss would pay the exorbitant rent.

He listened to the idea with a sidelong glance at me, then cut in:

"We'll do better than that, baby!"

I chose the furniture, drapes, and carpets. Driss bought knickknacks and a huge Japanese bed that took up the entire space of the bedroom. He gave me my first elephant, in ivory. Today there are more than fifty of them trumpeting into the Imchouk night, Imchouk, my cemetery of choice.

He never warned me that he was coming by, turning the key in the door without ringing the bell, to find me at the sink or stove trying out my own tajine recipes and creating new combinations of hors d'oeuvres. My hair bundled together in a large bright red or green scarf, dressed in a full and almost shapeless *gandoura,* I refused to let him touch me, cling to my behind, or bite my shoulder. Cooking allowed me to empty my head of its cesspool and to focus on something other than my wounds.

He ended up by understanding my rebuffs and was content most of the time to keep me company, quietly drink his wine, nibble his green olives and gherkins, tell me the city gossip, and explain the political changes, for which I had a modicum of interest.

Driss knew I didn't want him anymore but felt reassured when he saw that I still got as wet as before, a well-oiled physical mechanism that got going at the smallest caress. He would

penetrate me gently, dreadful show-off that he was, using half of his penis and making me balance on it.

"Don't be so mulish! Open your mouth so I can suck the tip of your tongue. Just the tip, my stubborn little apricot."

Of course, I came. Of course, he didn't ejaculate. Of course, I was thinking of Hamid. "I'm being cuckolded for a man," I would say to the mirror, a wrecked woman refreshing her lipstick after each of Driss's visits.

But leave him and go where? Driss had control over all of Tangiers. He was everywhere, shoving his cock even into the asses of men. I resembled a corpse after autopsy—the remains crudely fixed up with coarse thread and waiting to be pulled out of the morgue with a label attached to one toe.

I tried to explain it to Aunt Selma, who sent me on my way with a few sentences and a disdainful look.

"It surely was worth moving. That man turns up whenever he wants, sticks his nose in your business to be sure you don't have a lover. He jumps you between two orgies and sleeps when he doesn't give a damn about you. That monster has consumed your youth. He got you because he is a filthy rich city man, and the little peasant girl from Imchouk adores licking the aristocratic boots."

Licking, she said, saintly woman! I couldn't very well tell her that the man gave me an orgasm wherever he felt like touching me. Really! I was the stop where he got off.

"You do know, at least, that all it would take is a neighborhood creep to rat on you to the police for you to find yourself

inside?" Aunt Selma added. "But what am I saying? I forgot that madame is being kept by the most brilliant physician in the city, and she's untouchable. You say he loves you? No, my dear! The only thing *he* loves is his dick. And don't contradict me, or I'll knock my head against the wall!"

Does he love me, that man? Did he love me? I doubt it. Or only in his own way: casual, detached, desperate beneath his laughter, his impeccable elegance in gestures and clothes, his mastery over liquor, and his infinite, overwhelming culture, lighthearted in company and black-spirited as soon as he was alone, face-to-face with his own silence, whether or not he had a woman in his bed or on his arm.

Now I know why he could never fall asleep before he read *Le Monde*, which was sold in Tangiers with a week's delay; his classical Arab writers, whose brilliant and burlesque tirades he never tired of rereading; his American detective novels; and his French poets of the interwar period. Driss taught me to read. To think. And I wanted to chop off his head.

Yes, I finally understood: Driss's heart had no entrance. He was too solitary, loved stony landscapes, lives that had no rhyme or reason, minds that were lost and whose chatter furnished him with material for laughter and meditation.

I was wounded.

I was wounded and roaring in the cage of my head and couldn't suppress my rage. I refused to accept Driss's phone calls. I walked away from him when he took it into his head to meet me as I left the office. Every evening I would wash up, open the windows, bay at the moon, and make myself sick with insomnia, like a rat gone insane with mange, plague, or syphilis.

It was Aunt Selma who inspired me to find the right remedy, when I went to visit her three months after leaving her house in the Medina to move into the apartment in the modern part of town. My arms were laden with little presents, and my face was like a gravedigger's.

She talked about the weather, her toothache, the wedding of a neighbor's daughter. Then, in a firm tone and shaking her head, she concluded:

"Don't say a word. The doctor has told me not to get upset."

"I've made the decision: I'm leaving him."

"There she is again! You're leaving him to go and do what exactly? To go back to where you started from? Have you saved a few pennies, at least? Obviously not! And that pimp of yours? Has he given any thought to make sure you have a place to live? Would it kill him to buy you that apartment where he fucks you without any agreement or any witnesses?"

"I am not a whore, Aunt Selma!"

"That does it! My heart is racing, and my blood pressure is shooting up! Whores are paid by the session, you dimwit! He has been banging you for free for ten years! He is holding you in isolation. And don't tell me you're working! He just lets you catch a breath of air. Where is your leash, in fact?"

Her face tight, she added in a lifeless and detached voice:

"Make sure that your rabid dog buys you the apartment and puts it in your name. Do that for me. I want to sleep peacefully in my grave."

I wept. Aunt Selma's death was more than I could take. I couldn't even imagine her stretched out on the large board of the *maghssal* with a woman leaning over her body and washing her, reciting the Koran as she rinses the fair hair with attar-scented water, its macabre fragrance recognizable among all others. I didn't want to see her asleep and dead, a white woolen cloth around her hips to protect her private parts from the necessarily blurred vision of the woman washing her, although she would have seen many others. After the funeral ablutions are done, the woman would wrap her in an immaculate shroud, after stuffing her anus and nos-

trils with absorbent cotton. I didn't want to kiss her cold forehead and murmur, "Forgive me as I forgive you," before the body is raised and the women's cries and sobs, the men's '*Allahu akbar*' rise up. I preferred to ask her forgiveness immediately and tell her remorsefully, "I love you so much, Aunt Selma."

She stood up, took away the small low table that held our teacups, thereby indicating that the visit was over. As she went to the front door with me, she blew her nose and then, just as I kissed her on the temple, said:

"Remember that only a man is capable of cutting off the cock of another man. Go now, may God protect you."

The prescription was well known: Take another lover to avenge yourself on Driss. I woke up in my bed in the middle of the night, ice-cold, drenched in sweat, and completely lucid. Aunt Selma, I'll do better than take a lover.

I didn't need to ask Driss to put the apartment in my name. He did so of his own accord after I uprooted his cock from my head to hang it amid the wreaths of garlic and dried hot peppers decorating my kitchen walls.

I let a few days go by before seeing him again, playing dead, finding refuge at the house of a divorced colleague who was quietly leading a wild life and was paid in coin of the realm. When I did see him again, I was younger by ten years, had changed my hair, and was for the first time wearing the designer suit he had brought me two months earlier from Milan. He forgot to yell at me, feted me like a maiden, and covered me with new bank bills and music, imploring me to ask him for the moon. I asked him to have Hamid come from Fez and to invite him to dinner. Incredulous, he laughed:

"To do what?"

"Nothing. I just want to see what he looks like."

"You're going to fuck him?"

I took his question with a smile:

"After your two lesbians, I can be fucked at leisure."

He frowned. He stopped laughing. For the first time since I'd known him, he seemed worried, mistrustful of his creature.

"No, I don't think that's a good idea."

"Might you be jealous?"

"And why not? I don't want any men hanging around you."

"Hamid is not just a man. He's your woman, too, isn't he? I promise you I'll never fuck a woman, not without your consent, anyway."

"Fine, that's enough. I don't like it when you play the cynic."

"All I'm asking is to meet my rivals, male or female. You surely owe me that much."

Just for show he insisted:

"And what if I feel like jumping him?"

"Well, then I'll just watch you. That's the point I've reached."

For several weeks neither Driss nor I spoke about the idea again. I merely refused him my body, declined his invitations for dinner, and ignored his advances. One day on the phone, he shouted:

"I'm going to end up sticking it inside a donkey if you keep on neglecting me!"

"I'm sure the donkey will be delighted to allow you that favor."

He hung up, cursing.

Finally, he gave in. I received Hamid at Driss's house on the boulevard de la Liberté. Gallantly, he bowed over my hand, adjusted his tie, and said:

"I've been wanting to meet you for ages. Driss has told me so much about you."

Driss was not comfortable. He made do with grumbling a brief hello, served whiskey and rosé, lined up his Limoges porcelain bowls filled with green olives and pistachios, and then sat sullenly in an armchair.

"Are you scowling at me?" Hamid asked him.

"I'm tired. I had a terrible day at work. Three bypasses, one right after the other."

I murmured, "I've made pigeon pastilles. With grilled shrimp and cucumber salad as a first course. I hope you're both hungry."

They were not, and Driss was on his guard, watching both Hamid's and my gestures and looks. I cleared the table, and Driss served liqueur, lighting a cigar to go with his cognac. His mood was not improving.

I was doing the dishes when Hamid came in for ice cubes. Our fingers brushed each other's above the sink. That was all Driss saw when he came into the kitchen for a napkin, he told me later, at five o'clock in the morning.

He turned pale and pounced on Hamid, yanking him by the collar of his jacket:

"I forbid you to hover around her! You understand me, you fag?"

Hamid looked him straight in the eye for a long time, a smile at the corner of his mouth:

"Are you sick or what?"

"I'm a psychopath, a necrophiliac, a cannibal, and I'll fuck your mother if you so much as think of touching Badra. That one is mine, all mine! Mine, Monsieur Glans!"

Hamid dusted off his jacket, smoothed out his shirt collar, and, livid, retorted:

"And what exactly am I, according to you? I belong to whom?"

He left, rigid as a wounded cat. I dried the platters and the glasses, grabbed my bag, ready to leave.

"Where are you going? Who told you that you could leave?"

"Driss, you're being ridiculous."

"I don't give a damn! You move so much as an ear, and there'll be a bullet in your neck."

We spent the evening sitting across from each other in the living room, he gulping his alcohol and I counting the minutes. At midnight, I ventured to speak.

"I . . ."

"Shut up! I hate you, you slut! What are you thinking? That I don't know what you're cooking up, what you have in mind? Who do you think I am? Who do you think you are?"

"You've had too much to drink."

"I forbid you to talk to me, you viper! You want to cuckold me, is that it? Now that madame no longer smells of cow dung and wears Yves Saint Laurent, she thinks she can con me. Never! Never, I tell you! I'll put your eyes out first!"

He was unrecognizable, ghastly to watch. A complete maniac.

"You'll pay for this, Badra! Don't think you won't!"

He went to the kitchen, was gone for five minutes, and then came back with a laundry line.

"Get undressed."

I was wearing ocher-colored silk underwear and had my period.

"Don't even think of crying," he warned.

I had no intention to. I wanted to get this over with.

He tied my hands together and bound them to my feet behind my back. I accepted being beaten, raped, or both. He had told Hamid that I was his and his alone. Nothing else mattered. On the contrary, his rage was enough to set my soul ablaze.

My head was on the floor when he came toward me with a pewter plate. It held three glowing red and threatening pieces of charcoal. He always went further than I could imagine, always surpassed my fantasies and nightmares.

"This is what Touhami the farmhand did to Mabrouka when she dared to kiss me on the cheek at Grandmother's funeral."

He asked me to swallow the ember.

"Touhami, the farmhand, is not more of a man than I am! Touhami knew how to hold on to his woman. He knew how to train her. Open your mouth!"

I didn't hesitate. My chin and the tip of my tongue were burned. I am left with a slight lisp because of it that only a closely listening ear would pick up, but since no one listens . . .

He nursed me without untying me, turned me over, breasts in the air, then, as if I were a bride, carried me to the bed in his arms to lay me down. I didn't moan. I didn't protest. I couldn't speak.

So he spoke. And wept for hours. He banged his head against the floor and then against the walls.

"You want to leave me. Now I know you're really going to leave me. Why? Of course I'm crazy. Of course I'm a total loss. But, Badra, I love you. My mother abandoned me when my father had his accident in France on a rocky road near an inlet. And you want to do this again, do the same thing to me. You're taking revenge on whom and for what? Why don't you ever ask me to marry you? Why didn't you ever get pregnant by me? Why didn't I ever have the chance to let you have an abortion? All men have women. All I have is a cunt that drinks me and never says, 'Take me! Keep me just for yourself alone! Protect me from all other cocks and from the cruelty of the world.' Yes, you do say 'I love you,' but it is Egyptian-style, with honey and drums. I hate Egypt and piss in its crack! Love me the way you love your Harrath Wadi, you whore, and I'll marry you within the hour!"

Tell him that he had been my Harrath Wadi and he alone was all of Imchouk for me? Tell him that he had been all my men and women at the same time? Tell him that I'd never set foot in Egypt and am not an Arab as he believes but a pitiful Berber? Tell him that I don't know how to love him the way

he would like to be loved, and that he doesn't love me the way I would like to be loved?

Yes, we made love, in spite of my period. Yes, I sucked him halfheartedly, with my burnt tongue. Yes, I did come. Yes, he drank my wetness with small licks, at an angle. No, of course not. He didn't untie me. Before dawn broke, he simply stuffed the deed to the apartment between my breasts, covered with hickeys and bites. It had been in my name from day one.

In the street, my silhouette caused shop windows to reel. Men followed me, sometimes crude, often groggy with wine and sunshine. There you have it, I said to myself. They're running after their own death, asking to be decapitated with a blow to the jaw. A single blow. Tangiers smelled no longer of sulfur but of fresh blood.

After my breakup with Driss, I knew other men. Knowing is not loving—loving had become impossible for me. Unattainable. I didn't know that right away. Encounter after encounter, love thrust me like a phantom sex organ. Despite an amputated heart, I nevertheless continued to have perspiring hands and to buzz like a bee as soon as an encounter seemed positive, or a face sensitive, a set of teeth perfect, and a man vibrant and caressing.

Then it became more and more obvious that desire alone made me run away and suffer. Desire to play, kill, die, betray, spew out, and curse. To fuck, as well. To fuck like laughing, emptying a glass of water, or snickering in front of the spectacle of earthquakes and tidal waves. To screw

while not giving a royal fuck for the container. There wasn't one. The body doesn't exist. It is merely a painful metaphor. A trap. A magnificently boring and mortally repetitive game.

All the bodies I conquered like so many fortresses—two, three, several at a time, until empty, until infinite—could do nothing for me, just as I couldn't stop myself from doing it. I understood that loving was not of this world and that my men would leave my soul gaping forever, for lack of grasping that my vagina is its antechamber or preamble and that you cannot enter it the way you enter a bordello.

I got off whenever I wanted, free and unattached. Those who thought they were masters of my body were nothing but its tools, its playthings for one night, strong or less strong or weak alcohol that served only to shorten my nights and confound my migraines.

For fourteen years I was a slit. A slit that opens when touched. It made no difference whether the gesture was dictated by love, desire, cocaine, or Parkinson's disease. The fundamental point was that my head remained beyond reach, outside the playing field, that it recited dead poetry to itself, told itself racy jokes, or redid the monthly expenses. My head owed it to itself to remain firm, closed, and chaste while waiting for the body-partner, the body-mercenary, the body-stranger to head out the door and plunge into the night and its cold cinders.

I would go from opulent homes to the back-street shops of enriched merchants, from the depths of hidden recesses to risky dead-end alleys. Each time I entered the place of one of

my lovers, I had the stifling feeling of being behind closed doors and sealed windows. And, for want of opening them wide—for I was afraid of neighbors, passersby, vice squads, and the surprise visit of someone from my native village—I developed an exceptional instinct for identifying hidden outlets, the labyrinth of tiny alleyways that would take me across the Medina, whose convoluted layout resembled the picture of my adventures.

I traveled, too. Far and wide. I saw countries and discovered many customs at the expense of my lovers.

Invariably, I grow weary. Invariably, I get bored. Invariably, I dismiss them. Even the best-equipped penis is of no interest to me unless it brings me to orgasm. I don't give a damn whether they talk to me about Nasser or the bloodthirsty Hajjaj Ibn Youssef. I don't give a damn about politics, genetics, canon law, or market economies. Men talk, and I hold my fingers against my temples. I wait until they exhaust their word inventory and screw me at length, slowly, and in silence. As soon as my vagina stops slavering its pleasure, I turn my back to whomever has just given me cramps and orgasms. I don't give a damn about the gratitude of my lower belly. I don't give a damn about tenderness or postcoital sadness. I order my lovers to be silent, sleep, or leave. As soon as the door slams shut, I rejoice. I put on a jazz record or some Andalusian music. After midnight, I never listen to Arab voices; they stab me like knives. Even when they are silent, Arabs wound me. They are too close to me, too transparent.

I no longer count the mouths I've kissed, the necks bitten, the dicks sucked, and the buttocks scratched that clutter up my drawers today.

I have ample knowledge of the penis. Fat and lazy ones. Small and vigorous. Aggressive and lecherous. Clumsy and nonchalant. Mad, soft, and sweet. Tender and cynical. Scatterbrained and dishonest wanderers. Dark and tawny. Even a yellow and two black ones, out of pure gluttony.

Some made me weep with pleasure. Others made me laugh. One of them left me speechless because its size was so ludicrous. Another looked like an elephant's trunk, it was so huge. My vagina remembers them all, thinks of some tenderly but never gratefully. All they did was pay me my dues. Fortunately, I have long since forgotten any ideas of vengeance. Or else I would have cut all of them off.

Today, during his nights of pain and morphine, and unaware of the obscenity of his admission, Driss whispers to me, "I love you. I have never stopped loving you." I know that, and that is why I devote myself to pruning the rosebush and feeding the rabbits in their hutch.

He told me he tore his eyes out with remorse. He told me he cut out his tongue. My own no longer knew how to say I love you to anyone at all, other than to trees, turtles, and the faded dawns that rise just before I grow desperate to see the light again and hear the rooster crow. He told me he slit his throat, but it is mine that bears the scar.

When I left Driss, my broken heart did not wait to become multifaceted. By renouncing his face, I became prosaic, my ass within reach of the first comer—or almost—and, once the fooling around was done, not permitting my lovers to share my sleep, my ultimate citadel.

Another person's body is a desert. After a few years, they are all alike, whether it's the one I jerked off on the shore of Lake Constance or the one who couldn't penetrate me until we were on a cruise on the Nile. The one whose ass I almost ripped apart with a gigantic dildo or the one by whom I got pregnant twice out of carelessness. There was a time when I changed lovers with the seasons. A different one every three months. I would have liked a man to block the revolving door, to slow down my motor, too powerful for my framework. I would have liked to meet a patient man. For the impatient woman that I am, nothing is more impressive than people who know how to wait. But no one ever waited for me to calm down, to settle on his highest branch and begin to chirp. Men are in too much of a hurry, always speeding—eat, run, ejaculate, forget. In that, they resemble me, and I don't hold it against them.

Strangely enough, only a woman ever tried to cut through my protective crust. She had fallen in love with me without my knowing it, even before I touched her.

Wafa had the apartment next to mine at the time I lived across from the cemetery. She would often stop by in the

evening for some tea, a cigarette, and we'd listen to the records of Jacques Brel that Driss had given me just before we broke up. I was gulping pure whiskey and making rumbling sounds, too much in pain to speak, too inarticulate to put together a single sentence. She never asked me any questions, gazed at me lovingly, a virgin in love, already seduced, already abandoned. I always forgot to ask her to stay for dinner. I would forget that I had to eat myself. Over the course of time, as our wordless evenings, silent as the grave, ran together, she learned to prepare little snacks, then to do the shopping and make dinner without ever asking me for a penny or an opinion. She would do the dishes before going back to her forlorn young widow's apartment.

Then she began to do my laundry, iron my sheets and dresses. She became my little lamb, my sweeper, my lady's maid. Anesthetized by sorrow, I was blind to her misery and bewilderment. Since I refused to receive my lovers at home, I often went out and would see her light on when I came home. The following day, she'd look deathly pale with circles under her eyes and a bitter line around her mouth. She knew Driss, surmised the exact nature of my nightly escapades, and restrained herself from commenting on my behavior. She'd watch, wait, start when I happened to brush her shoulder in passing or absentmindedly rub my breasts when she was present. This went on for two years. Not once during that time did she confide in me. But her desire made such a racket that it seemed to me as if I heard an entire army of pots and pans going from room to room,

banging against the walls of my house. I chose to keep silent, undoubtedly out of exhaustion. Unless it was out of indifference. The indifference of those who have been badly burned.

One summer evening, while a hot wind crushed Tangiers with a leaden blanket, she served me a straight whiskey, did an about-face in the living room, and suddenly put her ice-cold hands on my nude shoulders. I didn't move.

"You know . . ."

"No, I don't. I don't want to know."

"Badra . . ."

She kissed my neck lightly.

"You don't know what you're doing."

"I'm doing precisely what I've been wanting to do since I got to know you."

"You don't know me."

"I know you better than you think."

"The wind and the lack of a male are making your head spin."

"My head has never been more clear."

"It's getting late. . . . You should go home and go to bed."

She slipped out, and I stayed behind, alone, to inhale the scent of the newly watered trees and the jasmine that wafted up, as obstinate as remorse. I was sad. I no longer had enough resolve to protect Wafa from her demons and my own. How could I tell her that I was nothing but a mirage? That I didn't exist? I knew she wanted caressing and love, which I was incapable of giving. That is all that the passing years are good for: sharpening a seventh sense that tells you immediately

whether a body desires you, whether a soul wants to drink you down to the dregs. I discovered I felt immense pity for Wafa, but inside my craggy landscape, there was no oasis whatsoever that could provide shelter, no hand to place some dates and a bowl of milk at her feet.

I didn't know how to tell her so, and she didn't know how to let go. Still, I didn't throw her out. Our once lifeless evenings together grew heavier with her thwarted fervor. I learned to handle her, hiding the smallest details of my body from her gaze, wearing roomy dresses that served me as armor, avoiding any posture that might be interpreted as an invitation. She silently laid siege to me. I held out wordlessly. This silent battle tainted the air and suffused it with a lovesickness that froze the stone I had for a heart.

She fell ill, struck down by a strange fever that gave her an aura of grievous beauty such as the madonnas have at the foot of the Cross. I prepared soups for her, put compresses on her forehead and temples, and changed her sweat-soaked sheets three times a day. A furious sun beat against the closed shutters, and my fingers and skin were wet with humidity. I needed a beach, salt air and cool evenings, but I couldn't abandon her in the desertlike, cruel month of August. She was holding me hostage, and I barely fought back, stuck in her dying woman's inertia.

After five days of being dismally shut up behind closed doors, I believe it was anger that pushed me to force her into bed and undress her with hands that allowed no protest. She

had heavy, milky breasts with pale pink aureolas and barely visible nipples. I took her left breast in my hand, my gaze in hers like a pin. Her eyes immediately filled with tears. She wanted to speak. I shook my head.

"Not one word. Not one gesture. You've put the rope around your neck, and I am the best slipknot you could ever find. Look at me. This is not rape. I don't want you. I don't love you. I am not your man, not your woman, and not your dildo. Nor am I like you. I'm granting you my poison, and just this once. The one and only time. If you insist, I'll decapitate you and bury you in your room underneath your bed. I want you to move, to disappear. I can't stand your widowhood anymore. Open your mouth, unclench your teeth. You're trembling. Don't press your legs together so tightly. Don't force me to beat you. You're wet with fear. How many years since the last time? How did he do it, that husband of yours? Straight to the target, two bangs and one premature ejaculation? Did he stick his tongue in your navel? Did he bite the inside of your thighs as I'm doing now? Don't touch me. I am not a penis. Don't look at me so imploringly. Are you opened up enough to let my fingers in? No. You're tensing up, and your breasts are jumping as I bite you. A bitter liquid is coming out of them. The same one that's making your sluggish pussy wet. Look at me. There'll be nothing more than an orgasm. I'm fucking you, and you'll never again bat an eyelash when people talk to you about brutal and stealthy lays. Stop acting like a praying mantis. Why did you have to get

infatuated with your neighbor who changes lovers every night and doesn't need your mournful sighs? Look. Now you're nothing but a puddle of female come. You're nothing but a gurgling vagina at my mercy. Isn't that what you wanted? You're heaving and want to snap me up inside your secret, shaking with panic, I see it underneath my hand that's taking possession of it. You're begging for mercy, demanding deliverance. I am not deliverance. I am your executioner of the moment, a moment that will get you off this instant through three different holes at the same time."

The worst thing was that she truly came.

My skin didn't touch hers at any time, nor did my mouth titillate her center of gravity. I screwed her without a shadow of passion, without a drop of tenderness, irritated that she had imposed her body on me, that she had used it as an alibi, a lame form of blackmailing death. I left her with her hair disheveled, half-naked, wrinkled, and wilted. I have never liked spiders. And even less the kind of people who inhale light and then refuse to relinquish it, planets dead before their time. Instead of fucking just to fuck, I prefer laughing and dancing, spraying from every pore, drinking straight from a cock, without batting an eye. I would have made love to Wafa if she had been sunny. But suns turn and don't roam the streets. Before leaving, I whispered in her ear, "Don't ever set foot in my house again." She moved two weeks after the episode. I hope she found a woman to love.

When Driss came to tell me he had cancer, I had already been around the world, amassed a small fortune, and changed addresses twice. At work I had moved up a few steps, and I was preparing my imminent retirement.

He said he'd never lost track of me. I didn't doubt that; Tangiers is just a big town where gossip crisscrosses. He said he had moved to a villa on the edge of a cliff, overlooking the sea, but I already knew that. "I'm asking you out to dinner," he suggested with a veiled look.

The city had changed since 1976, and for the most part our former restaurants had turned into real dives. Except for the Roseraie, whose terrace, set between two alleys of laurel roses, opened out onto the sea, lit up nightly by the backfire of the Spanish sunset.

Driss was driving a Mercedes. He asked me to take the wheel and was happy to watch the waves undulate under the first night breeze.

Fourteen years after our breakup, we apparently had nothing to say to each other, or very little. We ordered the same

grilled fish with french fries that we used to have. Egyptian pop music poured forth with deafening sound. Driss called the maitre d' and asked him to turn off "that shit music the old pharaonic harlot is forcing on us." I burst out laughing.

Usually, the old harlot was France and not Egypt.

"Well, now there are two," he snapped.

He wanted me to tell him what I'd been up to. I spoke to him of Dublin, Tunis, and Barcelona, of Vermeer and Van Gogh, of the erotic prints by Katsushika Hokusai. He sighed, "Ah, you please me so! You really please me! And I love your polish. Your perfume, too. Dior, if I'm not mistaken?" Then I told him about my impending retirement.

"I'm leaving Tangiers."

"Oh. . . . You're getting married?"

"No, just going back to the fold."

"I've heard about your mother. . . . Are you taking over the family house?"

"I'm buying out Ali and Naïma."

"You never liked Tangiers."

"That's not true. No city has given me what Tangiers has."

"Taken as much also, I would imagine."

"Oh, the city's not to blame."

I was breathing in the sea air, watching the outriggers float on the water in the harbor. Night fell sweetly, and the depth of the air was warm.

"I want to go home with you," he said.

Maternally, I shook my head.

"That makes no sense."

"I'm not talking about tonight. I'm talking about forever. I want to go home to Imchouk."

"You can't. It's not your home."

"You are my home. And I want to come home to you."

He told me about the metastasis, the morphine, and the final stage. My tears flooded the bream and the lime slices I had barely started on. All I had was a napkin with which to wipe them.

I looked up at the sky. What were we going to do?

"Badra, will you marry me?"

"Never!"

"You can't go back to Imchouk on the arm of a man who is not your husband."

"That's my business! Why didn't you ever marry?"

"For the same reasons as you, I suppose. Too much freedom, too much pride, too much everything."

We didn't speak of love. Or of the past. As we left the restaurant, Driss took my arm and leaned on it. My man had aged. From then on, he was my companion.

Driss came back to Imchouk with me to ask God for an extension or, if not that, to die in the wheat fields.

I look at him and barely recognize him. He sits near the window in the house of the *hajjalat,* our new home after the flood. He contemplates the sky and says he can hear the desert wind blow inside his chest. I go over to him and hold his head against my breasts. He kisses me through the fabric, then steals a kiss at the neckline. His hair is no longer as thick as before but still smells of fine water.

Night falls. I admire the Big Dipper and see stars fall. I didn't tell Driss that I saw Sadeq again, the first man to guide me, the stranger, through Tangiers. Sometimes I tell myself that I killed Sadeq and that I belong in hell, with God still mourning the death of a young man of twenty-four, mad and full of good manners. Nevertheless, God knows that I didn't see Sadeq fall and that I had not understood a thing about his unhappiness.

Sometimes he appears to me near the well, at the median where the north meets the west, where I say my prayers. He

always comes between the moments of *asr* and *moghreb* in the prayer, his face youthful and his silhouette grown frail. He knows that at that time it is forbidden to pray. He never talks to me, just watches me contemplate the sun as it goes down. In the beginning, he would weep. Since I have begun giving alms specifically dedicated to him, he is happy to escort me to a few steps from my door, ten minutes before the sun disappears behind the mountain. Even in death, he has remained jealous and proud. He refuses to cross the threshold of a house where a man other than he himself lies sleeping.

Since he has arrived in Imchouk, Driss directs himself to God without pulling any punches: "God, Beautiful and Great as you are, let me screw my wife again. Just once. Make her say 'I love you' again. After that You can send Your angels for me, and I will not protest."

Driss's throat may be eaten up with cancer cells, but his voice comes back when he talks to me or when he prays, for he insists that his crazed tirades are prayers. Sitting in the courtyard with a light blanket around his shoulders, he always starts off gently, as if he is chanting. The Harrath Wadi stops running, and the frogs stop croaking. The stars are copious, and at that point the dog is so full of milk curds that he doesn't even open an eye and snores like a Negus.

"God of the butterflies and elephants, You know I am worthless. You gave me Maari, Abou Nawas, Jahiz, Mohamed Ibn Abdillah, Moses, and Jesus, and I didn't know how to be grateful. You even gave me Oum Koulthoum, but that didn't

stop me from being an asshole. You gave me Voltaire, Balzac, Jaurès, Éluard, and all the others whom You know. You gave me the Nile and the Mississippi, the Mitidja Plain and the Sinai. You've inundated me with wine, figs, and olives. And I didn't know how to be grateful. Lord of the World, You also know that I have done worse things: I turned my head when Salome received the head of John the Baptist as ransom. I treated Lazarus like a madman because he let himself be resuscitated. I did not console Mary at the foot of the Cross, and I did not defend Mohammed when the kids of Thaqif threw stones at him. I did not defend Al-Hussein when he was surrounded in Karbala, nor did I offer him a gourd of water to quench his thirst. And I listen to Mozart without a single charitable thought for those lynched in Alabama. Lord, do You remember Alabama? Lord, have You forgiven the massacre of Deir Yassine in Palestine and the one of Ben Talha in Algeria? Because I, I have not forgiven that. Yes, Only God, True God, I have sinned. But . . . but . . . I have never offended a virgin or rebuffed a beggar. I have never allowed swallows to be thrown out of their nest or trees to be cut down so that those insane statements that insult Your intelligence can be printed in Arabic. Of course, I am no model for any one of Your creatures. I shouldn't have touched any fire, breasts, cunts, or Hamid's penis and behind. But do not add it up, Lord of the World, do not count. You know how I despise grocers! I look at the tree. I know. I hear the thunder. I know. I inhale the earth after Your rain has passed. I know. I

taste the blackberries. I know. I touch the skin of a woman. I know. Why did You make me blind, leprous, paralytic, and deaf to Your song? Why did You make me human when I would have been so much more beautiful as a stone, a donkey, or a music score?"

He falls silent for a few minutes, then picks up again, addressing the palm tree, which stands serious though somewhat aghast in the courtyard.

"Fine, You did make me, and I'm not going to remake You. Nor am I going to wave in Your face the sick I patched up who went straight to Mecca as soon as I fixed up their hearts. No, petty I'm not. Forgive me, Lord! Forgive me, but never forgive Badra! I don't mind dying. I don't even mind suffering. But Merciful God, make Badra know that I have loved only her and that as my last dwelling I want only her body. By the glory of Mohammed and Jesus among the mortals, tell her that I am already in hell for having spat on her love! I am dying. Dance on, frogs! Rejoice, woodlice! Daub your ass with henna, sons of whores!"

He wanted to make love to me, assuring me he could still get it up just as well as before, but I refused. "Do I disgust you? Does my breath stink, perhaps?" No, Driss. You didn't disgust me. But I was afraid you wouldn't find my breasts as firm and my buttocks as shapely. I was afraid that the flesh on my arms was quivering a bit and that you'd find the hair on my pubis whitened with age. I was afraid you would suddenly grow slack when faced with the body you had celebrated so much.

Driss used to say that women don't bury anyone. So I buried him. He used to say he would die against his will. Yet he didn't protest when the imam put a pinch of soil in each nostril and lay him on his side facing Mecca. I didn't wash or kiss him, for fear he would revive. I watched the gravediggers fill his tomb without protesting. All I said to the imam was:

"You know, he is going to kiss me as soon as you've turned your back!"

"Glory to God, the Only and Merciful God! Let him rest in peace! His body has left this world, but his soul has not renounced desire! We are only water and clay. May God have pity on His creature."

It is true that he never left me again. Sadeq no longer comes. He has understood that only Driss, taking his time, patiently and laughing, can explain to me how the stars function and how fig trees are fertilized.

I was writing when I sensed a presence behind my back and saw a flash of light go across the room. A scented breath brushed my temples. And a face bent down to read over my shoulder.

I didn't move. I didn't raise my head to identify my visitor, convinced it was the Angel. He comes back, probably subdued and more curious about my confidences than about my charms.

I heard his voice for the first time. It was reading my own sentences: "My life has been a succession of furtive embraces and forbidden coitions. I didn't have a grain of ambition, was not absorbed in the destiny of my people, and even less in the future of the world. Until the day I met Driss. After that, I never loved again. Not for lack of affairs. Quite the contrary. I would go from opulent homes to the back-street shops of enriched merchants, from the depths of hidden recesses to the most elegant palaces. Lucid, cheerful, or indifferent. Never in love again. Each time I entered the place of one of my lovers, the idea of closed doors and sealed

THE ALMOND

windows would oppress me. I exchanged my daytime hours as dutiful typist for nights as intrepid lover. Darkness became the casket of my adult body, whereas, when I was a child, I loved frolicking about in the light more than anything else. Then I thought I was forgetting Driss."

The voice spoke the secret of the handwritten pages. The privacy of my body and the subtlest of my emotions. The atypical course of my life. The mischievous child I had been and the Arab geisha I became. The incantations of faith and the obscene words. And my love for Driss. Eternal, imperious, and irascible.

At the bawdiest chapters, I felt the tonality change while at the same time something hardened against my back. I turned around and discovered the swelling. An angel's sex organ? I credited that to my fantasies. Nobody has managed to examine the anatomy of God's sweetest offspring. And experienced as I may have been in that area, I couldn't swear to it. I went back to my previous position without seeing the face of my guest. Then I heard his voice, this time full of disdain:

"Aren't you ashamed of what you've just written?"

Without budging, I answered:

"All you had to do was not read it."

"I didn't have any idea of the gravity of your errors." And then razor sharp:

"Now you'll pay."

I started:

"But you are an angel. That is not your role . . ."

"Not a single one of God's creatures would tolerate hearing so many obscenities out of the mouth of a woman."

I turned around. And suddenly I saw gigantic balls hanging down and a penis jutting out that resembled Chouikh's donkey's in every detail.

I examined the four corners of the room. In vain. There was no one. Except for only Driss's shadow, stuck in the doorway, and his voice murmuring, "Oh, my almond! You shouldn't be surprised. Get this into your head once and for all: When faced with the sins of a woman, angels are men like all the others."

Glossary

Adoul: religious notary.

Ajar: the fabric that covers the lower half of the face.

Al hamdou lillah: Praise be to God.

Antariyyat: heroic gesticulations, referring to the legendary hero Antar ben Chaddah, renowned for his physical strength.

Aoudhu-billah: May God protect us.

Babouches: traditional open-heeled footwear with a very pointy toe.

Baldiyya: urban elite.

Bendir: a percussion instrument.

Bint el hassab wen nassab: young girl of a good family.

Bismillah: in the name of God.

Burnoose: a long, hooded cloak.

Chorfa: descendants of the Prophet, considered to be noblemen.

Daya: a word of Turkish origin that refers to a woman of a certain age, a relative or a companion lady.

Dirham: a unit of currency. Thirty dirhams equals about U.S. $4.

FLN: the Algerian National Liberation Front.

Fqih: a master of religious science who is a marabout but also a charlatan.

Ghassoul: a clay-based body wash and shampoo.

Guiblia: a room that faces north.

Haïk: a cotton or linen veil worn in certain regions of North Africa.

Hajjalat: originally meant "widows," but in some regions of Morocco it refers to women of easy morals.

Harira: soup with a base of meat, lentils, and chickpeas.

H'bibi: a male friend or lover.

Houri: one of the maidens that in Muslim belief live with the blessed in Paradise.

H'ram or *haram:* illicit.

Jazia: the heroine of the Hilalian epic, famous for her long and opulent hair.

Khama: a piece of fabric like the *ajar* that hides the lower part of the face.

Lalla: a title given to older or middle-class women, equivalent to "Madam" or "Ma'am."

Maghssal: a kind of platform on which the dead are washed.

Melia: the traditional dress of rural Maghrebian women.

Moulay: the equivalent of "Monsignor." It is a title granted to highly placed personalities, superior clergy, saints, and marabouts.

Moussem: originally meant "season" but currently means the gift that is offered to the fiancée at Eid or on a saint's day.

Mtaqfa: refers to a girl whose hymen has been tied or "armored" so that she will not be deflowered before her marriage.

Ouliyya (plural: *oulaya*): refers to a woman in general and implies a woman without any defense or protection.

Qamis: a women's or men's garment that resembles a long shirt.

Saroual: baggy pants worn in North Africa.

Sman: rancid butter.

Swak: dried walnut bark, used to clean gums, whiten teeth, redden the lips.

Tahhar: the man in charge of circumcising male children.